SURVIVE OR DIE

It was too late to wish there'd been more time to select the ambush site. Tracer fire walked up the field toward Sergeant Hyde, and he barely had time to claw into the earth before splinters of wood and chunks of bark flew over his head.

Then he heard a more ominous noise—a loud, punching crackle of a sound he knew all too well. From the rear of the Russian convoy soared fat orange gobs of tracers. Faster and faster they came until they slashed at lightning speed through the dead timber around him.

The first rounds came the closest. But Hyde knew that with a 23mm flak cannon joining in from somewhere along the smoke-shrouded rump of the column, the odds had suddenly changed . . .

ACTION ADVENTURE

SILENT WARRIORS (1675, $3.95)
by Richard P. Henrick
The Red Star, Russia's newest, most technologically advanced submarine, outclasses anything in the U.S. fleet. But when the captain opens his sealed orders 24 hours early, he's staggered to read that he's to spearhead a massive nuclear first strike against the Americans!

THE PHOENIX ODYSSEY (1789, $3.95)
by Richard P. Henrick
All communications to the USS *Phoenix* suddenly and mysteriously vanish. Even the urgent message from the president cancelling the War Alert is not received. In six short hours the *Phoenix* will unleash its nuclear arsenal against the Russian mainland.

COUNTERFORCE (2013, $3.95)
Richard P. Henrick
In the silent deep, the chase is on to save a world from destruction. A single Russian Sub moves on a silent and sinister course for American shores. The men aboard the U.S.S. *Triton* must search for and destroy the Soviet killer Sub as an unsuspecting world races for the apocalypse.

EAGLE DOWN (1644, $3.75)
by William Mason
To western eyes, the Russian Bear appears to be in hibernation—but half a world away, a plot is unfolding that will unleash its awesome, deadly power. When the Russian Bear rises up, God help the Eagle.

DAGGER (1399, $3.50)
by William Mason
The President needs his help, but the CIA wants him dead. And for Dagger—war hero, survival expert, ladies man and mercenary extraordinaire—it will be a game played for keeps.

Available wherever paperbacks are sold, or order direct from the Publisher. Send cover price plus 50¢ per copy for mailing and handling to Zebra Books, Dept. 2633, 475 Park Avenue South, New York, N.Y. 10016. Residents of New York, New Jersey and Pennsylvania must include sales tax. DO NOT SEND CASH.

CIVILIAN SLAUGHTER

James Rouch

ZEBRA BOOKS
KENSINGTON PUBLISHING CORP.

ZEBRA BOOKS

are published by

Kensington Publishing Corp.
475 Park Avenue South
New York, NY 10016

First printing: April, 1989

Printed in the United States of America

FOR CELIA.

A war crime is a breach of the laws or customs of war.
—Dictionary definition.

The only crime in war is getting yourself killed.
—Sergeant-Major Patrick Wilson.

It is only a war crime if it is discovered.
—Colonel Boris Tarkovski.

When we do it, it's an operational necessity. When they do it, it's a war crime.
—Peter Manteuffel. Journalist.

All war is crime.
—Pacifist leaflet.

Chapter 1

"But Comrade Commissar, my orders . . ."

"Screw your orders." Colonel Tarkovski reached out and gripped the corner of a filing cabinet to steady himself. Vodka slopped from the tumbler in his free hand, running down his wrist to soak the cuff of his soiled jacket. "Your tanks stay here until I've finished with them. Understand?"

"Yes, Comrade Commissar."

The young tank major of the Soviet 3rd Shock Army offered no further dissent. It would have been pointless and dangerous to argue with a senior officer, especially one as drunk as the colonel, but literally suicidal with one who also wore the insignia of a KGB political officer.

"Then clear out and have those clanking wrecks of yours do that little job for me. When my battalion pulls back I don't want so much as a scrap of used toilet paper to be found by the NATO troops."

"They will find nothing of value, Colonel."

"I don't care if they get their hands on the treasures of the Kremlin." Tarkovski swilled the contents of the glass around, watching the last struggles of a large fly in the clear alcohol. He drained it, without bothering to remove the insect. "What I don't want them to find is evidence of a little going away party held by me and my men. Now get on with it."

Ignoring the tank major's salute, Tarkovski replenished his glass. He did so from a near empty bottle that stood on a long table crudely improvised from oil drums and rough planks. Setting the bottle down again, he had difficulty finding a space for it among the clutter of chains, wire, and tangles of stained rope. The unplaned timber was further littered with sticky heaps of pliers, metal shears, and knives.

The heavy chemical-screen curtain at the entrance to the dug-out had hardly ceased flapping from the major's abrupt exit when a junior sergeant entered.

"What do you want?" Almost losing his balance, Tarkovski lurched a half step sideways and collided heavily with the cabinet. Its top drawer slid open. He slammed it hard shut but it opened again.

"All the other bunkers have been cleared, Colonel. Shall we remove this equipment now?"

Absently Tarkovski rippled his stubby, dirt-ingrained fingers along the tops of the exposed close-packed index cards. "Yes, you may as well. Have it put in the back of my field car."

The sergeant waved two men into the room and they began to gather up the tools. One of them reached beneath the table and lifted onto it a large truck battery. From its terminal posts trailed long leads that ended in rusted crocodile clips. It was heavy, and he almost dropped it.

"Watch what you're doing, shithead." Dribbling saliva as he snarled, Tarkovski glared at the soldier. "You, I can replace in minutes. Good batteries take forever."

"Shall I have the bodies removed, Colonel?"

"Hmm?" Making the effort to switch his bleary focus to the corner the sergeant indicated, Tarkovski took a moment to collect his thoughts. "Oh, them. I'd forgotten them."

The naked body of a middle-aged man was sprawled in contorted fashion on the tamped dirt floor. Masses of burns, deep cuts, gouges, and contusions showed on his pallid and slightly blue-tinted flesh. His wrists were almost severed by the fine wire tightly binding them, and his eyes were gone. Wedging open his toothless mouth was a piece of splintered timber and filling the cavity between the bloody gums was a ragged wad of torn tissue and matted hair.

Beside that corpse hung that of a woman. The razor wire by which she was suspended from a hook in the wall had bitten deep into the skin beneath her arms and across the tops of her big breasts. The tips of her toes just brushed the floor.

She had been a disappointment to the colonel, a great disappointment. He'd had his eye on her for weeks, had been saving her. Then, when she'd witnessed a little bit of routine work before her own turn, she'd thrown up, and choked. He'd tried to save her, shoving his fingers down her throat to clear the obstruction, but it had done no good. She had drowned in her own vomit. Her bladder had emptied all over him as she'd died, but that thrill was small compensation for the loss of what he'd actually been looking forward to.

Even in death she'd still managed to spoil things. First washing her down with vodka and crumpled pages from *Pravda,* he'd tried cutting her, but she'd hardly bled. When he did things to them he liked to slide about on their blood but even that had been denied him. He'd had to finish himself off by hand, be content with doing it over her.

"Shall we remove them, Comrade Colonel?"

Putting off a reply with a negligent wave of his hand, Tarkovski squinted into the open drawer. Riffling through the dog-eared cards he finally extracted two. Slowly and deliberately he tore them into tiny pieces and let the scraps run through his fingers.

"No. No need to bother with them. They do not exist any more."

Chapter 2

The tree line was a wild tangle of broken branches, interspersed with splintered stumps and the battered empty cases of cluster bomb dispensers.

Sergeant Hyde's squad had dug themselves in along the fringes of the war-ravaged woodland. Several times he had walked out into the open to check their concealment. At last he'd been satisfied with their camouflage and they'd settled down to wait.

There was no movement, no conversation. Each man was encased in the private stifling world of his respirator and NBC suit. Laid mostly in individual shallow holes, they were so still that even from close up there was little to reveal that they were not just another small group of forgotten bodies, left over from some minor action.

A rare slight movement as a cramped muscle was carefully flexed, or as a fractional adjustment of position was made, to further improve a field of fire, was all that there was to betray that they were not corpses.

Before them the ground sloped gently down toward

a long straight stretch of Autobahn three hundred meters away. The road surface was sprinkled liberally with the craters of direct hits by bomb, rocket, and shell, and smothered in soil and lumps of clay thrown from near misses in the fields alongside. At irregular intervals, sometimes singly, sometimes in small clusters, stood the fire-seared wrecks of trucks and trailers. All rested on their axles, tires burnt away. Most had been reduced to virtually unidentifiable condition. Only the occasional outline of a partially intact cab gave any clue as to their origin.

On the far side of the broad highway, flat meadowland had become a sodden morass where drainage ditches had been obliterated by a carpet of explosives. Gradually sinking into the cloying mire were the flame-ravaged hulks of a troop of T88 Warpac tanks that had attempted to escape the carnage on the road. Their thick composite armor had offered scant protection from top-attacking terminally guided munitions. Now, minus tracks and every external fitting, even turret and gun in one case, they were gradually disappearing into the mud. They were taking with them the charred remains of the crews.

But it was not the pounding and the churning of high explosives that had killed every last blade of grass in the fields. After that violent tilling the soil had been drenched with toxic and defoliant chemicals. It was those ugly, indiscriminate weapons that had crudely sterilized the land.

In the remains of a drainage ditch alongside the Autobahn the still water was colored not with the green scum of stagnant growth, but with the life-leeching taint of a cocktail of chemical agents.

"We're in business." Sergeant Hyde gave Dooley a jab with his elbow. He pointed to where indistinct dark outlines were beginning to emerge from the smoke-filled air a kilometer away.

Swinging the thermal imaging sight of the Milan rocket launcher to bear, Dooley was able to make out the distinctive bulk of a heavy truck, and then more as others followed it into vision. "All right! I owe you fifty marks."

Without taking his eye from the target, Dooley reached out. His gloved hand patted across the two-round reload case to check it was unfastened. No matter how much they wore the all enveloping NBC suits it was never possible to become completely used to them. They made every action clumsy, restricting vision and hearing and communication. Even the cologne doused muffler he kept tucked inside couldn't mask all the other odors from the long hours, sometimes days, they were forced to wear them. He'd have given anything to rub his eyes, scratch his nose, but that meant lifting the respirator, and that was out of the question. The contamination monitor strapped to his wrist was showing a reading almost off the scale. Contact with any twig or stone, or any unfiltered breath could prove quickly lethal.

The drifting perpetual pall that so reduced visibility in the Zone had been thickened in this sector in the last month by non-stop battles, as the NATO forces had maintained pressure on the retreating Warpac forces rear guards.

Dust and smoke had combined to the point where now, at midday, it reduced the orb of the July sun to a blurred orange patch. That was the only relieving color in the otherwise monochrome landscape.

"How did you know that they'd be moving equipment by this route? They've a dozen to chose from in our patrol area." Dooley had the cross-hairs aligned dead-center on the lead tractor unit of the approaching convoy. He had only to make fractional adjustments to track it as it steered a slow cautious path between the craters and the litter of wreckage.

"The Reds have kept their forward airstrips in use until this morning." Hyde made a mental note about the fifty mark bet. It was always difficult to collect from Dooley. Most likely he'd end up having to add it to the other three hundred already outstanding. "Airlift capacity is too stretched and precious to let them haul out graders and dozers that way, but a complete airfield repair battalion is too valuable to abandon. So I figured they'd make a run for it close to the cease fire, when our gunships would be back at base. This route is the most direct and being metalled it's not as chewed up as some."

Lifting his head from the Milan, Dooley made a quick scan of the rest of the column. While the lead elements would soon be level with their position, the tail end was only just emerging from the fog. He counted ten slab-sided tracked towing vehicles, as many trailers bearing heavy plant and several huge-wheeled power shovels and multi-wheeled cranes. Mentally ticking off the squad's weapons, even adding in the Milan's reloads, he knew they didn't have the fire power to do telling damage to so many large targets. Sergeant Hyde must have been thinking on the same lines, as he sighted down the barrel of his SA80.

"Pity we can't call down artillery. Any request for it now is going to be referred all the way up."

"And all the way down will come a 'get your fingers off the trigger' type order." Switching the sight to normal vision, Dooley could see the Russian driver of the lead truck laboring at his heavy steering. Beside and behind him sat other drab NBC suited men. They sat motionless, like ugly dummies.

"You're all too right." Hyde checked the time again. "We're cutting it fine. I make it thirty minutes. No staff officer is going to stick his neck out at this late stage, not for any target."

Not for a moment did it occur to Dooley to ask why they were, that wasn't the way the squad operated. They just got on with the killing. They were very good at it. They'd had a lot of practice.

For him at this moment it was enough that his back was itching and driving him mad just where he couldn't reach it. He welcomed anything that would take his mind off it.

The convoy had slowed to an agonizingly slow pace. Hyde could see a distinctive blemish on the lead vehicle's front wheel. He watched it, mesmerized, willing it to rotate faster.

So close to the deadline for the cease-fire, the Russians obviously thought themselves immune from attack. Another couple of kilometers to go, and then they'd be safely into the Warpac side of the intended demilitarized territory.

Mentally he urged the Soviet driver to put his foot down. Gradually the rest of the transports had begun to bunch behind him as impatience overcame convoy discipline.

The long line of prime movers and semi-trailers snaked between the clusters of rusting derelicts. Hyde searched among them for any armor or towed weapons, but found none. There were, though, several tarpaulin-shrouded loads that could have been automatic weapons of any caliber. Several of the trucks' cabs had anti-aircraft machine guns mounted above them, but none were manned.

"They're worried about time as well." Hyde heard the blare of a klaxon.

About halfway along the column, dwarfed by the machinery about it, a command car was trying to overtake. A figure leaning out of the open passenger door was making sweeping urgent gestures.

The Russian officer must have been looking at his watch, and worrying. His concern, though, would be a different one entirely. A principal clause in the published truce terms was that any military equipment remaining in the cease fire area after zero hour must be immobilized and abandoned. A Warpac commander who allowed that to happen could expect, at best, to be demoted to the ranks of a disciplinary unit on mine clearing.

The message was obviously understood. Immediately the Zil eight-wheeler in the lead began to pick up speed. Its powerful twin engines plumed black fumes from its high mounted big-bore exhausts.

Over the sights of his rifle, Hyde tracked it as it neared the skeletal remains of a radio truck. The Zil's stake-sided load deck was crammed with men, so many that the press appeared to be bowing the wooden rails outward.

It was doing about thirty when the road erupted

beneath its cab, between the first two pairs of wheels. A tongue of flame drove up through the billowing cloud of smoke and debris and engulfed it.

Chapter 3

The roar of the mine explosion reached the tree line as the Zil emerged from the smoke. Front end collapsed on broken axles, it ground great sheets of sparks from the road. Flames were already licking from the shattered windshield and engine hatches.

As it slewed to a halt, the sides restraining its human cargo snapped under the weight of bodies thrown violently against them, and a flailing cascade of men toppled to the road.

With short precise bursts Hyde swept the load deck clear of the few who had kept their balance. That done, he hosed a whole magazine at the Russians seeking to crawl and drag themselves to safety beneath the canted chassis. The sudden eruption of a fuel tank engulfed those who made it.

Blocked by the wreck, the remainder of the convoy slammed to a halt and their crews bailed out. Several stumbled, or fell and lay still, as other lines of tracer from the woods targeted them.

Its arcing flight marked by its vivid tail-flare, the first of the Milan missiles swept over the broken ground and impacted dead center on a stalled tractor unit. A fountain of white and silver globules of molten metal marked the point of penetration.

The missile was designed to defeat the thickest armor to be encountered on Warpac main battle tanks, and the sheet metal of the tracked vehicle offered virtually no resistance. A shaft of vaporized metal and explosive bored deep into the engine compartment. Instantly there spouted from the entry point a gout of bright yellow fire and a blazing figure tumbled from the cab, followed by a red bubble of fuel-fed flame.

"What do you want me to take out next?" Dooley snapped the first reload round into place and panned along the convoy.

Using the last of a clip on a command car that was trying to maneuver around the pyre the Zil had become, Hyde took in the effect of the squad's fire. It was frustrating, there were so many juicy targets and they hadn't the weight of ordnance to do a thorough job.

"Hit another of the tractors. If we can't smash them all, we'll bottle up as many as we can."

About to turn his attention back to the command car, Hyde saw it rock on its suspension as a rifle grenade detonated immediately above it. Peppered by the storm of fragments, it shot backward out of control, a bloodied head lolling from a side window. Without check to its gathering speed it veered on an erratic course, cannoning off a gutted radio truck and hurtling over the edge of the Autobahn. A wall of discolored water hid its roll into the ditch, to be instantly replaced by spurting steam.

The foul fumes from the launcher's first stage ignition percolated through the filters of Dooley's respirator. He held his breath against them as he kept all his attention on his selected victim.

Its main motor failed to fire correctly and the Milan swooped toward the ground trailing a dangerous telltale stream of thin white exhaust. Barely skimming the surface of the field there was no chance of the projectile reaching its intended target and Dooley shifted to the closest available. A towering six-wheeled Kraz mounting a squat hydraulic crane—even that proved too far.

Pancaking onto the Autobahn, the missile broke up and threw a sheet of burning warhead material and rocket propellant in a broad fan over the scarred concrete.

An erratic scattering of automatic fire was being returned now, much of it converging on the aiming point offered by the Milan's betraying plume of smoke. In the still air it hung like a faintly accusing pointer to its source.

Tracer walked up the field toward Sergeant Hyde, and he had time to claw into the earth before the last few rounds of the burst punched deep holes in the lengths of bough heaped up before him. Splinters of wood and chunks of bark flew over his head.

Then he heard a more ominous noise. A loud distinctive punching crackle sound he knew all too well. From the rear of the convoy soared fat orange gobs of tracer. Faster and faster they came until they slashed at lightning speed through the dead timber around him.

Those first rounds came the closest, but Hyde knew that with a 23mm flak cannon joining in from somewhere among the smoke-shrouded rump of the column, the odds had suddenly changed.

It was too late now to wish there'd been more time to select the ambush site. Their transport's turret-mounted Rarden cannon would have been more than a match for the enemy weapon, but placing it among the jagged woodland would have been impossible. The spears of flayed timber would have ripped the hovercraft's tough ride-skirt to shreds and disabled it more effectively than a direct hit.

Despite the casualties and damage they had inflicted, the Russian unit was largely intact and there was little more they could do. Bitterly Hyde blasted off two full magazines in quick succession toward the mobile crane, but the massive truck appeared to soak up the beads of tracer without harm.

"Use the last round. Any target. Just make sure of a hit."

Dooley had already reloaded, and as he fired could only hope that another malfunction would not signal their precise position. "No go. It's dead."

"So are we if we hang around until that cross-eyed Red gets better on that 23mm. Is that thing safe to cart away?"

"Can't swear to it." Machine gun bullets punched two holes in a log beside Dooley. "They have been known to go off after a hang fire."

"Leave it, then. Pass the word to move out." Unclipping a phosphorus grenade, Hyde waited until he could see the others were clear before moving back into deeper cover and lobbing the chunky cylinder beside the Milan launcher.

He didn't wait to see it ignite, but ran crouched low

to catch up to the others. A seemingly solid stream of cannon tracer slashed through the woods to their right. Several of the rounds found still standing trunks and split them with giant cleaver force, and sending scabs of bark high into the air.

Almost up with the others, Hyde saw a man go down ahead of him. He recognized Thorne's distinctive Tiger-stripe helmet cover.

"I'm OK, just tripped. Oh shit, oh bloody shit." There was a long tear in the leg of Thorne's protective suit. The material under it had also been ripped and speckles of dark blood were already forming on a long graze.

"You'll be OK." Unclipping the sling from his rifle, Hyde bound it about the man's thigh to pull the fabric together. "You've taken all your shots and pills?" It was a question he hardly need ask. They were all too well aware of the likely consequences of not doing so to overlook the regular dosing with nerve-gas antidotes. "Keep moving. We'll scrub you down as soon as we get back."

Behind them, despite the obscuring smokescreen, the Russian fire was growing in volume. Spent bullets fell about them. When they started down a steep reverse slope to the fold in the terrain where their transport waited, the sounds of the blind retaliation were suddenly reduced. Only a rare stray blob of ricocheting cannon tracer served to show that the Russians were maintaining their profligate expenditure of ammunition.

The air-cushion armored personnel carrier sat low on its collapsed ride skirt. Its camouflage paint blended in perfectly with the dead birch trees among which it was parked. As they approached, its raked bow door lowered and they entered by the ramp it formed.

Last to board, Thorne collapsed in the opening. Gloved hands grabbed at his webbing to drag him in, but were pushed aside by the sergeant.

"He's gone. We'll have to leave him here. The body's contaminated."

"I'm not fucking leaving him to rot." Dooley stepped over the still figure. "Someone give me a hand."

Ripper dived out past the NCO and helped the anti-tank man to lift Thorne onto the starboard engine pod where they wedged him among the spare ride-skirt panels. A few turns of loose rope around the legs and waist of the corpse made sure of its staying there.

"You're bloody ghouls." Hyde plugged into the intercom circuit as he took his place at the command position across from their driver.

The door silently closed and then there was only the pale illumination from the instrument panels and that reflected through the periscopes down each side and from the vision blocks in the command cupola.

"What's the heading, sarge?" Burke only asked as a matter of form. He'd already taken the turbofan engines to full thrust and was setting a course back for their base.

"How are we for time?"

In the turret Clarence heard the sergeant ask, and withdrawing the clip of proximity fused anti-aircraft shells from the compact breech of the Rarden, substituted three armor-piercing instead.

"I make it ten before . . . why?" A suspicion jumped

into Burke's mind. "If you're thinking what I think you are, Sarge . . ."

"Don't think, do. Take a right, circle the woods, all the speed you've got."

Dipping under the surge of acceleration the HAPC skidded through a tight turn with its nose down and a shower of dirt thrown high to mark its progress.

"I want a maximum effort." Though it made no difference, Hyde turned to look back down the interior as he said it. "There'll only be time for the one pass. I don't expect us to be taking any ammunition home with us."

Ripper thought of Thorne's body, flopping and bumping against the hull, arms and legs outstretched, as though crucified. That's what they'd all be if somebody's watch was slow. "We're gonna be ever so deep in the shit if the brass find out about this, Sarge."

"Well, the only way they'll find out is if the Ruskies kick up a stink and fix it on us. Let's make sure there aren't too many witnesses."

Moving at top speed the hovercraft rolled and swayed in a sickening ship-like manner. The automatic ride height sensors failed to respond fast enough to the rapid changes in terrain as they crossed patches of bomb cratered landscape.

Like the others, Dooley had turned to man a ball-mounted machine-pistol. He almost lost his balance as the craft lurched and canted over on another violent change of heading.

Above him the Rarden opened up with an earsplitting crack that was hardly lessened by the respirator, or the continual hiss of static over the intercom. Bracing himself against the jolting of the wild ride, he waited for a target.

There was a series of tremendously loud bangs and the craft shuddered as it took several impacts. All Dooley could see through his periscope was giant orange tracer skimming past so close he didn't think it possible they could miss. Then three more struck the turret, and their gun went silent.

Chapter 4

"What's the problem?" Hyde had only a second or two in which to decide whether or not to abort the attack. They were still racing straight at the rear of the convoy. The brief respite from the surprisingly accurate Russian cannon fire could only be because they were reloading.

"I've fixed it."

As proof of their gunner's word, Hyde heard the Rarden punch a measured trio of shots toward the trailer mounted flak-gun. The first shot went wild, the second was closer, seeming to strike the tow-bar joining the trailer to a light truck. The third impacted immediately below the 23mm barrel at the moment it began to reply.

There was a flash, unaccompanied by smoke and then the enemy weapon elevated skyward and loosed a long burst into the air.

Knowing he must have got the gunner and probably the elevation mechanism, Clarence took his time over the next shot. Waiting for a smooth patch of ground where the range was point blank, he put two shells into the mount from the flank.

A feed belt or magazine ignited and hid the cannon and the remains of its crew inside a sparkling cascade of brilliant white and blue flame.

One or two of the convoy's machine guns chased the hovercraft with long bursts, but their attempts to bring their weapons to bear failed as they underestimated the attacker's speed. Several others were still firing at the tree line and made no move to switch their fire to the real danger.

If they even recognized it, they left it too late. Crossing the ditch where it was nearly filled by rubble from craters, the dashing hovercraft seemed almost to take off as it leapt onto the Autobahn behind the last vehicle in the convoy.

A captured Land Rover with slapped-on Warpac markings, it was actually reversing to get away when the HAPC sideswiped it. The impact spun the Rover through 360 degrees, hurling its driver onto the road. Before he could scramble to safety a ripple of machine gun fire from a side mounted weapon aboard the hovercraft virtually cut him in two. Another burst riddled his late transport and started a blaze among cans of grease and oil in the back.

"Look at them run." Dooley had all the targets he could hope for, or cope with.

A hundred meters on the far side of the road Burke put his machine through a right angle turn to bring it on course parallel with the stationary transport. With speed reduced to jogging pace they travelled slowly the full length of the convoy.

Suddenly aware they were caught on what they had thought was the safer blind side of the road, the Russian soldiers panicked, some dying as they collided with each other in their rush to find new places of safety.

With steady precision, shells from the Rarden 30mm cannon were pumped into the motors and fuel tanks of every vehicle and piece of plant and machinery. Under the ferocious impacts, cylinder blocks were cracked open and fuel, cooling and electrical systems smashed and shredded. Fire sprouted instantly and tractors, trailers and loads alike were engulfed by infernos of flame.

A group of Russian field engineers had taken shelter beneath the bed of a large compressor. Oil poured over them as a solid shot ripped open the motor's sump. They became torches as an incendiary shell burst and ignited the spillage.

Other human targets were sought out by the armored hovercraft's infantry passengers, and brought down by swirling cones of automatic fire as flames flushed them from hiding.

Using the roof-mounted grenade launcher, Hyde sent salvos of anti-personnel and smoke bombs at the road. Scything fragments and eruptions of white phosphorus added to the death and destruction.

"That's it, job's done." Hyde shouted to their driver. "Get us out of here fast!"

As they raced from the scene, Hyde set the bomb thrower to lob decoy devices in their wake. Noise generators tumbled into strident life on the ground. A screening pall of hot smoke was created by the sequential detonation of a mass of sub-munitions. Bursting in the air, each short lived fiery-centered cloud could draw off any missiles homing by infra-red emission detection, while masking them from observation by any thermal imaging sight.

Traversing the turret, Clarence took a last look at the convoy before the smoke concealed it from view. From a rapidly increasing distance it appeared as if a full half kilometer of Autobahn was a continuous sheet of red and yellow flame. An impenetrable curtain of black smoke rose high above it, blotting out the pale sun.

"The Reds will create a stink over this."

Through the thick, clouded prisms of the command cupola, Hyde took in the scene. He heard their gunner's words, but made no reply. It was done, irreversible. Only now did he remember to look at the time. He couldn't be certain whether or not they had continued the one sided engagement beyond the cease-fire deadline. Well if they had, he'd be hearing all about it soon enough.

"We must have copped a bit of damage." Burke was having increasing trouble keeping the craft on course. "I think the ride skirt's taken a hit. We're spilling air."

"There's a railroad overpass two kilometers dead ahead." Hyde checked his map, though he had hardly any need. They had fought over this area, to the east of Hanover, many times before. "Take us down into it. Turn south, there's a road bridge, we'll tuck in underneath it. No point in advertising where we are."

As the hovercraft nosed over the edge of the embankment and slewed sideways down to the track bed, they became aware of a steady leathery drumming against the left-front of the hull. The machine had taken on a definite and uncorrectable list to that side.

"Must be that Land Rover that got in the way." Burke examined the chunk of aluminum. "Looks like a part of his wheel arch."

"I don't give a damn if it's a part of the driver's crotch." Hyde surveyed the ride-skirt. "How long to replace those panels?"

Burke shrugged. "Maybe thirty minutes. Quicker to do both than mess about patching the one that's still hanging on."

"I want it done in twenty." Hyde reached into the craft and pulled a Stinger missile from under the driver's seat. "Give me a whistle when you're ready. And for Christ's sake do something about him." He indicated the body entangled with the components Ripper and Garrett were trying to free. "Cover him over."

Looking from the Stinger the sergeant held nonchalantly, Burke found himself involuntarily scanning the sky. "No chance of us being pounced on, is there? The truce is in force now, isn't it?"

"Why take chances? I'll be up on the bridge. Remember, twenty minutes."

The bank was steep and with his awkwardly bulky load Hyde was sweating profusely by the time he reached the top. He threaded his way through the rusted remains of a wire fence and walked to the center of the bridge.

A wrecked West German civilian ambulance and a couple of well bleached skeletons stood at the far end. The vehicle's front was crushed flat where it had been bulldozed aside by a tank. He hoped that the knocked out T72 in the distance was the one that had done it. Both tableaus dated from the first days of the war.

Then the Warpac forces had rampaged across this part of West Germany. It had seemed like nothing could stop them. On the first day, heedless of losses, they had made forty miles in places. Hyde remembered being at a HQ the first evening, seeing the red flags sprouting on the situation map as Russian reconnaissance elements and Spetsnaz units turned up in places they had no right to be, far behind the NATO front line.

But as the markers of NATO units had been steadily moved farther and farther west and grown steadily fewer in number, although they weren't to know it, the Warpac advance was already in deep trouble.

It had been a totally unexpected factor that had first dislocated and then stopped the pell-mell assault. Soviet satellite troops, mostly Polish and Hungarian but with a few East German also, had mutinied.

Months later, when NATO forces had begun to recapture odd pockets of territory, they had come across mass graves. In one Hyde had counted over a thousand bodies in the top layer alone. The stench had driven him off from completing even that crude estimate. But not before he had recognized the uniforms.

The pit had contained the rotting remains of a whole East German infantry battalion. Slaughtered to a man, with no pretense of selection or discrimination. Officers, drivers, medics, all had been mowed down and dumped like so many bags of garbage.

Since then they'd seen countless other examples of the Communist way of instilling loyalty and discipline. What an ugly farce it made of all the disarmament talk of the 1980s. All of Gorbachev's "glasnost" had counted for nothing when the Russian military chiefs judged it had gone too far and taken over the reins.

There was no real danger of their coming under air attack. Hyde had used that as an excuse to get away on his own for a few minutes. He could hardly believe that this truce meant the end of the war. There had been five others before it, none had lasted more than a couple of weeks. The average was six days.

But if it was, what then? When the war had started he'd dreaded a disabling wound. Well, he'd got a disfiguring one, and now because of it, he dreaded the peace.

The chemical level indicator was registering a low reading, he took off his helmet and lifted his respirator. Flakes of graft tissue came with it, adhering to the straps.

Thorne had been unlucky to pick up something so deadly, even on that poison-riddled tract of land. But he'd been lucky not to have suffered. The pain didn't have to continue for you to suffer from a wound.

With the tips of his gloved fingers Hyde pressed the spongy tissue of his face. There was no sense of feeling, in the same way as he had no sense of smell or taste. All that had gone in the fire, with his face.

From below in the overpass came the stuttering note of a klaxon, and he started back. At the fence he paused, sighted on the T72 and sent the missile on its way. It was a direct hit where the turret sat on the hull.

Where was he going to use that skill in civilian life? It was a joke. For him there was only the war. For him it had to go on.

Chapter 5

From the roof of the hotel Major Revell had a good view of the grounds and the countryside for several kilometers all around.

The battles that had surged back and forth had largely spared the impressive old building. A couple of solid shots, tungsten-tipped misses from a distant tank versus tank engagement, had punched holes in the walls and a single five hundred pound iron bomb had cratered the garden and destroyed the serried precision of much topiary work, but that was all.

Even looting had been on a very minor scale. It was a good choice for the Special Combat Company's base. Close enough to the rear bases to enable Carrington and his team of brilliant scroungers to prey on the dumps, and too far forward to be of serious interest to higher commands who might otherwise have appropriated it for themselves.

Beyond the perimeter fence had sprung up the inevitable clusters of refugee tents, huts, and shelters. Wisps of smoke rose from them, and the copses nearby already showed the usual sprinkling of fresh stumps where fuel had been cut.

Lieutenant Vokes climbed out through the skylight and joined him. They watched as a pale blue Jaguar XJS executed a high speed dry skid in through the tall wrought iron gates at the far end of the long drive.

Twin fans of gravel marked the sports car's savage acceleration and it fishtailed slightly on the loose surface.

"Andrea?" Vokes admired the vehicle's handling as it left the drive and tore across the overgrown lawn to be lost from sight among the wide spaced lines of military vehicles parked beneath camouflage netting.

"Who else? She's developed a passion for the exotic. It was a Ferrari yesterday."

"Where does she find them?"

"There are some big houses tucked away in these parts. I suppose most had two or more cars. When the civvies pulled out they were more likely to take the Rolls or the Range Rover. Can't carry much in a Ferrari."

"True." Vokes sighed. "I must say, I wish it was me she had her small warm hand around rather than a gear shift."

"Take my advice, don't try it. She's capable of pulling either out by the root." There was a time, not long before, when Revell would have jumped on any one talking about her like that. But he'd changed. What he had felt for her she had burned out of him. "Garrett was the last to try. He was wearing his balls in a sling for a week. He's scared witless of her now."

The Jaguar reappeared from between a pair of dapple painted Saxon wheeled APC's. It made a high speed hand brake turn onto the drive, shredding thousands of miles from the tires, and rocketed back out onto the road.

As the roar of the high revving motor died away it was replaced with another familiar sound. The distinctive thumping beat of a Huey grew steadily louder.

Vokes shaded his eyes and looked in the direction. "Twin door guns. That will be the colonel, will it not."

"That I could do without. What does Ol' Foul Mouth want with us?" A thought struck Revell. "Where's Hyde and his squad?"

"Still in decontamination, over by the lake."

"Right, keep them there, or at least out of the way until you see that chopper lift off again."

Not asking or waiting for an explanation, Vokes hurried back down from the roof. Revell followed at a more leisurely pace, mentally equipping himself for the trouble he was expecting.

The colonel was stalking into the lobby as he reached the bottom of the elegant staircase.

"What the bloody blue fuck are you up to, Major?"

Revell waited for the first blasts to wash over him. He knew from experience there was no earthly hope of having his say at this stage.

"Shit. I get you boys a nice easy number in a quiet sector, so you can build up to strength again after your last blood bath, and what do you do? I'll tell you what you do, you near get me busted all the way back down to civilian convict. And seeing as I start as a full-blown colonel, that's a piss awful long way."

"Is it about the patrol?" Revell thought it best to determine that up front. The colonel had been known to spring the odd surprise by blowing up over a less than obvious matter. But this time Revell had it right.

"You call that a patrol? A patrol?" Colonel Lippincott extracted a sheaf of photographs from his pocket and waved them above his head. "With a runaway regiment of maniacs in kamakazi tanks I couldn't have stirred more shit than you've done with one lousy APC."

"Is that a compliment, Colonel?"

"That is not a damned compliment, and it wasn't when I got it in exactly the same words from a two-star general. Have you the faintest idea how much work went into laying on this truce?" Lippincott waved any potential answer aside. "No, course you haven't. Nor have I, but you can bet your ass it was one hell of a lot. And so while all along the Zone, from the Baltic to the Med even the most head-banging gung-ho bomb happy shit is cheerily putting aside his rifle and taking up knitting, you go out and try to queer it for everyone, and me in particular."

Face red, Colonel Lippincott paused for breath. "Let's get some air. This place stinks like a stale morgue." Not waiting to see Revell tagging along behind him, he strode through the overturned tables of the opulent dining room and out through the elegant conservatory on the back of the building.

Broken glass crunched under their boots. As they stepped out onto the broad terrace a light breeze wreathed them in wood smoke and they moved to the far end to get out of it.

"Just what the blue blazes is that guy doing?" Lippincott pointed to the long shallow pit in the middle of the lawn. Tending the red-hot filling of wood ash, and replenishing it constantly from a nearby stack of logs was a sweating smoke-stained figure in grubby shorts, army boots, and chef's hat.

"That's Scully, the company cook."

"Is he not used to civilization?" Lippincott jerked his thumb over his shoulder to the hotel. "Back in there must be one hell of a catering kitchen. Does he always do things the hard way?"

"We're having a barbecue."

Resignedly Lippincott sprawled on a stone bench. "Of course, I should have known. One minute you're fucking up the truce, next you're having a sing-song around the campfire."

Revell was waiting to see the photographs. They were becoming gradually more crumpled in the colonel's grasp. "So is it . . . fucked?"

"See for yourself."

They were aerial shots, with the slightly grainy effect that showed them to be unenhanced frames from a sequence obviously taken by an RPV. All ten were of the convoy ambush. It was the recorded time printed in white in the top left-hand corner of each that interested Revell most.

"See the HAPC in some of the shots? Know whose it is?"

"I'm not denying it's ours, Colonel. We've got the only one in this whole sector. I presumed that was why we were chosen to carry out patrolling up until the last moment."

"Precisely my damned point." Accepting the return of the prints, Lippincott crammed them into the breast of his jacket when he couldn't get them into his pocket. "You were to patrol, not do a cannon-armed simulation of the caped crusader at work. Who the hell told you to cream that Russian outfit?"

"Nobody said we couldn't." Absently Revell watched their cook dragging a soil encrusted tree stump toward the pit. "Those timings, on every picture, show my men turning away before zero hour for the cease fire."

"Yeah, but thirty fucking seconds. I've been in action, Major," Lippincott waved the empty sleeve of his jacket. "You can't tell me that in the middle of a red-hot action your vehicle commander was doing some sort of crazy NASA countdown."

"Whether he was or not, they finished in time. Are the Russians complaining?"

"Don't they always; never known a people for belly-aching like they do. This time, though, you got lucky. Again. As we were flying in I heard over the radio that the Swedes who are policing the truce caught some of the sneaky sons of bitches trying to extricate supplies after the deadline. That about makes us even by all accounts."

"So why the visit?" Turning, Revell half sat on the stone balustrade. He knew there had to be more coming. The colonel was very much a hands-off commander, only made special visits for special reasons.

Taking a pencil from a top pocket crammed with them, Lippincott began to chew, keeping up a spitting hail of pieces as he gradually reduced its length. "You know your outfit isn't liked by the big chiefs. They're still beefing about 'private armies' and dilution of resources. If I didn't get you the odd mission too mucky for the Guards or the Air-Cav to tackle . . ."

"Seems like all our tasks are like that."

"As I was saying, if I didn't volunteer the Special Combat Company for a few of the more distasteful jobs I wouldn't be able to justify your existence. Right now, though, they're after blood. I've made my peace by saying we'll do penance . . ."

"I get the feeling most of it is going to be done by my men."

"What the hell do you expect?" Lippincott pushed himself to his feet with the stump of his arm against the back of the bench. "You knew the form. You were around for the other truces, you know how fragile the damned things are. Only takes one stupid mistake and it's total war again. We need this breathing space. Sure, we've been chasing the tail of the Reds for five weeks, they're on the ropes, but I tell you, so are we."

Revell remained sitting as the colonel stalked back and forth on the neatly interlocked slabs of soft-colored sandstone. "The men reckoned, I do, that one last push and we'd have had them back over the East German border, maybe well on the way to their own."

"You don't see it, do you? All you've got is your own little slice of the action. To the top of the next hill, the end of the next street, that's your war. Well it's bigger than that, there's a lot more to it." Lippincott snatched out one of the photos.

"This Russian engineers outfit you burned up. How many of the vehicles used to be ours? Three-quarters? It's usually around that isn't it. Of course it is, without captured equipment they'd have been back to horses and carts a long time ago. Come to that, some of their units are already. So are some of ours. The Zone is the biggest battle of attrition the world's ever seen, bigger than you can ever imagine from the little bits you see. Another week, maybe less, and more than two thirds of our armor would have been immobilized by lack of spares or ammunition or both."

"That bad?"

"That fucking bad, and worse. The West German airforce has almost ceased to exist as a viable combat arm . . . Same goes for the Brits'. Every Harrier that comes off the line is issued immediately. Some go into action unpainted. You must have seen that for yourself."

He'd seen it, but never realized the full implications. Their small battle group was almost self-sufficient, replenishing itself by battlefield salvage. It had given him a false impression of the overall picture. "So how many Hail Marys are we to do?"

"By the time it's over you'll wish it was that simple." Lippincott dabbed at his eyes as an engulfing cloud of wood smoke made them water. "Let's walk, before that chef of yours has us first on the menu as smoked hors d'oeuvres."

They picked their way past a solitary bomb crater, skirting tangled heaps of uprooted and wilting hedges. Revell made a point of steering a path away from the lake. Just audible was the whine of the pumps serving the decontamination sprays.

"It might not be for long, of course." Lippincott glanced sideways at the major. "Depends on how the cease fire holds up."

They reached a boundary fence, reinforced by entwined razor wire. Beyond it the heathland stretched away in a series of gentle folds. In the middle distance stood an isolated stand of fir trees. Farther off a few scattered rooftops were just visible.

Close alongside the fence was a huddle of improvised refugee shelters, looking as if they would all collapse if any one wall were removed. Sitting on either side of a small fire consisting mostly of cones and twigs, an elderly couple were taking turns to spoon beans from a can.

They ate slowly, savoring every mouthful. When the hot can was passed from one to the other, elaborate care was taken not to spill anything from the cloth wrapped container.

Revell watched them, wondering if the food came from the company's reserve stock. He noticed a clean bandage about the woman's wrist. That would be Sampson's work, and tended to confirm the source of the meal. "So what will we be doing? Riding herd on a load of these poor devils as they're shunted around the countryside?"

"No," Lippincott looked away from the scene. It was too common to hold his attention for long. "No, you're going to be riding shotgun on a load of Russians."

Chapter 6

"My men will be wasted as prison camp guards." Even as he felt his anger rising, Revell knew protest would be useless. Instead, his mind switched to considering the first problems which would arise from such a change of assignment. First and foremost would be the need to keep a careful watch on Andrea and Clarence. Both had a self-imposed vendetta against the Communists. It was hard to say which of them was the most ruthless in its pursuit: Clarence with his merciless sniper's precision or Andrea with her less cool but just as deadly blood lust.

" . . . it's not quite so simple, Major." Spitting a last fragment of wood, Lippincott selected another pencil. He crunched off the eraser and nibbled thoughtfully at the paint down one side, like he was sampling a doubtful stick of celery.

"Of course we're all hoping the cease fire will become permanent, but I guess there's not many who believe it really will. Leastways none of the staff officers reckon it's likely to make it into a second week. So, in exactly the same way as those bastards on the Warpac side will be doing, we're going to get ourselves ready for the next round."

"Is there that much we can do?" Revell moved aside a little to give the barrage of soggy splinters more room.

"You bet your fucking life there is, as long as we stick to our side of the demilitarized strip. There're dumps to be replenished, defense positions to be constructed and improved, material to be salvaged and roads to be repaired . . . especially roads."

Revell could anticipate what was coming. His anger, being pointless, had subsided, to be now replaced with a sullen resentment. It was going to be worse than guarding the cages. "We take charge of a construction battalion? Of Warpac deserters?"

"Got it in one, almost. Only you're not getting some easy-going bunch of Poles and Hungarians. In fact you're getting all Ruskies. Not to dress it up for you, you're getting the sweepings of the camps. All the ones who've been causing trouble. The guys who refused to work, or were into stealing, murder, or gang buggery, or trying to dabble in the black market by bribing guards. You know, just about every vice known to man, and some that are only known to renegade Communists."

"Where do we find them."

"Oh, they'll find you. They're on their way, be here about mid-morning tomorrow. Your company will take over as their escort for the last stage of the journey. I should think the other guys will be glad to hand them over to you. Did hear they've already had to stop twice and put MPs on board to sort out knife fights."

"What's the work precisely, and where?"

"Clearing and patching a section of road that runs up

to the truce line. Goes right on through it and into the Warpac side, in fact. If you keep out of the demilitarized strip though, you shouldn't have any trouble from that direction. The escort commander will give you a map."

"What about engineering equipment?" Inside Revell was a strong suspicion that he already knew the answer to that also.

"Each of your new buddies, gallant allies or filthy traitors depending on whose point of view you're seeing them from, our PR boys or the KGB, comes fully equipped. To be fucking precise, with either a pick or a shovel."

"Sounds like it's going to be a bundle of laughs."

"Well the general was smiling a hell of a lot when he gave me the word. Now I've got to be getting back. Can you offer a route back to the chopper around that clown producing the smoke screen."

Lippincott belted himself in, while Revell stood at the open door.

"Great, ain't it." The colonel tapped the back of the empty pilot's seat. "OK, so this machine's not exactly new, maybe hardly airworthy, and sure as shit I'm not a three-star general in the making, but together we're a slice of the NATO war effort, and what happens? We come to a grinding halt because this crud has to scuttle off for a piss."

Revell, too, suddenly had strong feelings about the pilot's weak bladder, but not for the same reason as the colonel. There came a blast of rock music as a convoy of assorted civilian vehicles entered the grounds. Leading them was an ex-Warpac generator truck. Mounted on top of its box like bodywork were two enormous speakers. Following closely was a Rolls Royce convertible, a pair of Starstreak missile launchers sprouting from the place where the passenger seat had been. It and the rest of the column were heavily festooned with bright balloons and masses of bunting.

Corporal Carrington, seated on the back of the Corniche, created a temporary panic among the surrounding refugee settlements by firing off a whole belt composed entirely of multicolored tracer, then he waved to the officers.

Groaning inwardly, Revell experienced a familiar sinking feeling in the pit of his stomach. He saw the colonel, open-mouthed, watch the weird variety of impressed transport crunch over the gravel toward the hotel.

"They're just letting off steam. Celebrating the truce." Hell, even as he said it, Revell knew it sounded weak.

Observing a Toyota pick-up grind past in low gear, laden with a tower of cases of wine and beer, Lippincott curled his lip in disbelief. "The hell they are. This looks like it's building to be one of your parties."

From the open hatchback of a much dented Opel a dirty face appeared, bearing a leering expression.

"The girls are on the way, Major. Is your friend stopping? He'll have to get in line. There aren't enough to go round."

"Who the hell is that, one of the replacements?" Lippincott's glare had no effect on the disheveled PFC, who raised a can in mock salute before washing his face with its contents.

"That's Ackerman. He came highly recommended, by himself. Does have some useful contacts though. Some surprising ones."

"I can imagine, but I want to know what's going on."

Shrugging, Revell tried to make light of the situation. "Like I said, Colonel, a little celebration."

"In a fucking pig's eye. And what girls was that maniac going on about? Who could you get to come all the way out here, apart from a few of the whores from one of the cleaner camps, unless . . . " Lippincott looked at his subordinate with suspicion, and then as comprehension dawned, with something approaching awe.

"You've roped in Frau Lilly and that mobile brothel of hers, haven't you."

"I said Ackerman had some useful contacts. She's said she'll stop by . . ."

"Frau Lilly . . ." Lippincott lost himself in thought, "Why she and I go way back . . . but never mind. If you ever decide to get rid of this Ackerman, pass him on to me. I thought Lilly never obliged anything less than a Divisional HQ; a man like that could be useful."

"You're welcome to stay and join in the fun, Colonel."

"I'm sorely tempted, sorely, but not this time. I recall your last party. Dooley invited me to play football with him, I didn't know he meant with me as the ball. I was combing glass out of my hair for a week. And besides," Lippincott winced as "Bat out of Hell" belted out across the park, "I can't stand heavy metal."

The pilot returned, slowly, as he was continually casting wistful glances over the preparations. Reluctantly he climbed in, and began his checks.

"There's something else." Lippincott leaned out and

made sure he had Revell's full attention. "It's the general's orders. I've got to see they're carried out."

He'd been half anticipating there would be a sting in the tail to the colonel's visit. Revell saw his superior hesitating, but there was no way he was going to make it any easier for him.

"You won't like this, but with the truce on, the general reckons you won't be needing your armor. And before you ask, that means all the captured vehicles as well, and the HAPC. He figures if you're only riding herd on a bunch of unarmed Reds the personal weapons should be more than sufficient."

Above the cabin the rotors began to beat the air, drafting rippling patterns through the grass.

"One last thing." Leaning out, Lippincott bellowed into the major's ear to make himself heard as the engine ran up to full power. "Those aerial shots of your strike on the convoy—according to the photographic interpretation boys it looked like one of your guys was riding outside the HAPC. The general wasn't happy about that. Said it was crazy. Tell the madman not to do it again."

Over the colonel's shoulder, Revell could see the filled bodybag in the back of the cabin. "He won't, Colonel."

Chapter 7

"Am I going nuts, or can I hear praying?" Dooley stopped toweling his closed-cropped hair, and cocked his head on one side to listen.

"I don't know about going crazy, but yes, you can hear praying." Carrington lounged in the open doorway and watched Dooley hopping about as he struggled to pull on socks over still wet feet. "It's Old William."

"That ancient Dutchman with Vokes's pioneers? When did he get back? After the crack he took, I'd have thought they'd have invalided him out for certain."

"He hitched a ride with me, up from the dumps. Apparently he'd been hitching his way back, been on the road for the best part of a week. Certainly seems fit enough, for a bloke his age. Got what looks like a depressed fracture on his right temple you could put a golf ball in, but he seems all there. Not that he says a lot, mind you."

Dooley succeeded with the sock, and then swore when he saw that the heel was on top of his foot. He sat on the edge of the bed for his second attempt. "Come off it, how can he be all right in the head? Here we are, about to indulge ourselves in the wildest debauchery and greatest drunk of all time, and he's praying. And you say he hasn't got a screw loose? Anybody who at this moment isn't shining themselves for the party has to be a few bricks short of a full load."

"To each their own. As long as he doesn't hide the booze or try to convert my lady friends, I'm easy." Carrington looked around the room. It was littered with pieces of equipment, weapons, and wet towels. "For a guy who wants to impress the ladies, you haven't paid much attention to housekeeping, have you?"

"Ah, now that's where you're wrong." Clad only in his socks, Dooley opened a connecting door with a flourish. "This is where I'll do my entertaining." He was pleased to see that the corporal appeared suitably impressed.

"Very nice. Thick pile carpet, four poster bed, silk covers, yes, very nice. Hope you don't mind me saying though, if that's all the outfit you're going to wear, you don't think it might make you appear a little overeager to get down to screwing, do you?"

"Fuck off. I'm getting dressed, of course I am. I found some really cool threads in the staff quarters on the top floor, the attics. Had a bit of trouble finding anything my size though."

"See what you mean." Carrington watched him haul up and squeeze into a tiny pair of shorts. The printed pattern of entwined hearts bulged and creased to a series of distorted red blobs.

"You reckon the room looks OK? Haven't overdone it, have I? These girls are used to mixing with top brass, used to a bit of class."

"No, it's in perfect taste. The case of beer beside the

bed is a nice touch. Just the sort of thing they'd be expecting."

"Smart ass. That's for me. There's a case of champagne on the other side." From the window Dooley caught a glimpse of a strange vehicle entering the grounds. He thought his eyes were playing him tricks, and looked harder. No, he hadn't been mistaken. Three Warpac, eight-wheeled armored command vehicles were approaching the building. Each of them was painted a bright pink.

"They're here. The girls are here!" Immediately he grabbed up a pair of undersize Levis and struggled to get into them. "Wait for me, you shit." He shouted after Carrington. "Wait for me. Where are my bloody boots, wait for me!"

"It's no good you doing that." Dooley watched, head propped up on a pile of satin pillows, as the woman swung her heavy breasts from side to side across his body. "You've drained me."

She sat back on her heels and pushed empty beer cans off the bed. "Too much drink. It is not good."

"Not good? I've come three times already. I bet that's a couple more than those chairbound warriors you usually service."

"Maybe without the beer you could have been four times better, or perhaps five. Do you want to do something else? We can join some of the others if you like. That can be fun. Even if you only watch."

"I'm not into that group stuff. Tell you what I would fancy though, now that we've slowed down. How about an ordinary cuddle, no rude stuff."

He watched her. She was a tall, big-boned girl. Possibly in her mid- to late-twenties. Rising to a kneeling position straddling his legs, she ran her hands down her sides over the front of her thighs and then up between her legs.

"Open another bottle, and pour it into my hands."

The cork and its harness of twisted wire rebounded from a far wall. Hesitatingly Dooley poured the fizzing wine into the cupped palms she held out to him.

"Ah, it is so cold." She dashed the champagne over her belly and down into her pubic hair. "Again."

"I've seen booze used for just about everything, but not for washing down there."

"It is good. The bubbles, they tingle."

"What you going to do with the bottle afterwards?" To his surprise Dooley sensed his penis begin to stir, sluggishly.

The laugh she gave was deep, almost masculine, and she opened her mouth fully to make it. "Not for masturbating myself. The foil around the neck, it chafes too much. For that I would need Liebfraumilch bottle. Do you want me to find one? I thought you wanted to hold me. I have found that men do not always like it when I am sticky underneath."

"Stay here. You go out on those stairs, I might not see you again." He pulled her down and folded his broad arms about her. The talc they had been playing with earlier made the upper half of her body a strangely smooth contrast to the wetness lower down.

"Oh, and this is the big man whose first words to me were that I would do for the first of many tonight." She walked her fingers down his chest to rest her open hand on his stomach.

"Yeah, well we all shoot our mouths off when the others are nearby—force of habit."

"Hmmm," she nuzzled into his neck, fluttering her long eyelashes to tickle his ear. "You are much nicer when you are being yourself, like this. Will you be staying here for long?"

"Why do you ask? Are you a spy?" He was only half joking. The major had got them all together for a lecture before the start of the party.

"In a way, sometimes. Are you shocked, or surprised?"

"No reason why I should be. In the Zone we all do what we have to, if we want to survive." He found himself able to believe her, was somehow sure she was telling the actual truth. "Does it pay well?"

"The Russians are not good payers, or at least their agents are not. Hard currency is difficult for the Reds to get hold of, and many take a cut before I have my share. For a laugh some of the girls will make up information and then each tells her controller. Of course with so many different sources they believe whatever we have told them so the payment for that is bigger. Then we are paid again by the C.I.A. or M16 for passing on disinformation. It is fun, and there are few risks."

They had been together four hours, and this was the first time Dooley had really talked to her. Until this moment he'd hardly given a thought to what life she had beyond this bed and this room.

She was a lot younger than the women he normally battened on to when he was on leave. Not that he could always find someone who'd have anything to do with a soldier from the battlefields of the Zone. Fear of chemical or nuclear contamination or bacterial contagion kept many out of his reach.

He'd almost forgotten how smooth and silky a female's skin could be. How it could be full of curves that didn't sag, or bag and wrinkle at every movement in bed. Her hands were pretty as well, neatly manicured, with none of the veins standing out.

He brushed her hair aside and his hand brushed against the sharp petals of earrings. "Shit, those things are lethal."

She laughed, a subdued throaty chuckle that he felt vibrate against him.

"I do not like my ears to be touched, or bitten. I had those made from razor wire, and then gold plated."

The light from the arcs in the garden and on the terrace flooded into the bedroom as a breeze stirred the curtains. It brought the faint tang of woodsmoke.

Falling on her face, the light made her eyes glisten and sparkle. For the first time, after all those hours of intimacy, Dooley kissed her.

Chapter 8

The terrace was littered with bottles, half empty glasses and discarded scraps of clothing. Hyde picked his way through the party debris and turned off the generator. The lights faded with the throb of the engine.

Behind him, in one of the upper rooms a portable was blasting out the latest number one on both sides of the Atlantic. As though in sympathy with the sudden silence below, it cut off abruptly. A moment afterward it was replaced with an old Abba tape, and the volume appropriately reduced.

From deeper within the hotel came a scream that turned into a shriek of laughter and then a scream again.

Having kept out of the festivities by choice, Hyde had never felt more lonely. He went down the steps to the lower terrace, to lean on his hands against the back of a stone bench. It felt gritty, and slightly damp.

It was dark down here. He didn't have to make an effort to conceal himself, the night did that for him. When he heard footsteps behind him he stayed still, didn't turn around.

The steps, woman's steps, came closer, and he heard the light rustling of a dress and caught a faint aroma of a musky perfume.

He ached. Out the corner of his eye he could barely make out a dim outline, although she was only a few steps off. Though he'd seen most of the girls as they'd arrived, he wasn't able to recognize her. It was he who wanted to, but it was she who spoke first.

"You have not enjoyed the party?"

"No, I'm not much of a one for parties. How about you?"

"It was a long drive here. I am not a good traveler, so I have been resting."

"So you haven't . . ." At that point he had to stop. He was saying the wrong thing. How could he say "so you haven't fucked then?"

"Not yet, no."

What else could he say. Could he ask a hooker if she was enjoying her night off? He sensed she had added the word "yet" quite deliberately, but her tone had given nothing away.

"I know what you are thinking."

As she spoke she played with a light scarf, short impatient gestures with it, drawing it fast through her fingers so that the material slapped against them.

Hyde pressed himself against the back of the bench, feeling the unyielding sandstone biting into his erection. "What am I thinking then?"

"You are thinking all of the questions that men so often ask. Like how many have I had, do I ever enjoy it or do I only pretend to. Those sorts of questions."

"Well, do you enjoy it?" He could feel his penis beginning to leak. There was a creeping dampness inside his clothes.

"Yes, sometimes it is good. Being with Frau Lilly means that everything is always well-organized. That means we can feel safe. Not on edge all the time. It is better if you are relaxed."

There were more near hysterical screams from the hotel.

"That will be Jackie. A new French girl. Always she makes a lot of noise."

"Do you have, sort of a regular boyfriend, as well as . . ." He was saying the wrong things again.

"Frau Lilly discourages that, but some of the girls have. Mostly the men are posers, free-loaders. Always they expect presents."

"You don't have one then." Not that Hyde cared one way or the other. He asked her just to keep her there. For a while longer to have her to himself.

"There will be time enough, when I have put sufficient money away. Perhaps though I will not want anyone. Or like two of the older girls I might prefer to live with a woman. I have never done it with a woman, but I can imagine it, I think. It would have to be a pretty girl, not one of those smelly tweed-wrapped sacks of potatoes who try to be men."

It felt like he was going to burst. He backed off the stone or he would have come, simply from hearing her talk of such things. The thought was in his mind of how he could grab her and take her right here. Even if she protested, fought him, it would be over so quickly that he could get away without her having seen enough to identify him. But that wasn't how he wanted it. A thousand times before this night he'd wished a similar fate on the unknown Russian gunner who'd destroyed his face. He was wishing it again now, with every fiber of his being.

In the darkness, perhaps there was a chance, they were all but invisible to each other. No, anything might happen, a beam of light from the hotel, the arcs being switched on again. Worse than not starting, to have her yell with fright when she saw him while they were doing it.

"How are you feeling now?" His mouth was dry, he had difficulty forming the words and they came out as a hoarse whisper.

"You mean you want me."

"Yes." He had been nodding like an imbecile for a minute before he could produce the word.

"Do you want to do it here?" She took his silence as "yes." "The ground is hard, and this is a good dress. Do you like to do it standing up."

Christ, he'd have done it standing on his head. He wanted so much just to ram himself inside here, but he had to be careful. He didn't want to frighten her off. "Can I do it from behind?"

"You don't want to do anything dirty do you? I don't like that. It makes me sore for days."

"Oh no, no." He struggled for the right words, had heard the disapproval in her voice. "I want to be able to touch you at the same time."

"All right then." She lifted her skirt and hooking her thumbs into the waistband of her panties, eased them down and stepped carefully out of them, not letting them touch the ground. "But no tricks. If you try to put it in the wrong place I shall be angry, and go back to the bus."

"Whatever you say. I'll do whatever you want." And Hyde meant it. At this stage of frustration and anticipation he'd have done absolutely anything for her. Even go down on his knees in front and lick her until it soaked him. So long as at some stage she let him penetrate her and stay in her body until the release of the urgent pressure that was making his groin red-hot.

"I am ready." She braced herself with her feet apart, palms resting on top of a low wall. The silky material of her underwear cushioned her left hand. "Pull my dress right up out of the way."

In the darkness he had moved behind her and she felt hands bunching her clothes up over her waist. She tensed as the damp tipped warm hardness of an erection slid over her bottom, then relaxed as it moved down and began to urgently probe between her legs. Bending forward slightly she reached down and guided it in. There was a groan behind her and she felt the man's body shuddering as he penetrated as far as he could.

Her skirt wedged up between their interlocked bodies, fingers slid over her hips and glided gently over her belly to explore among her pubic hair.

Despite herself, her unwritten rule, she knew she was going to come. As she felt him climax she pushed against the wall to force his fingers to greater pressure and then she was gasping and moving uncontrollably as well. "Again. Do it again, the same way."

Hyde's breath was lung-hurting gulps of air, like a man who had surfaced from deep under water. With hardly any break to the rhythm of their movements he started again. There was a sudden commotion from the hotel but he paid no attention to it. All there was for him was the woman and what they were doing together. Nothing else mattered, nothing else existed.

"What the hell."

The thud of the explosion was right over Revell's bed, and was accompanied by a shower of ceiling plaster that transformed him and the girl to white apparitions.

He'd got used to the yelling of the woman in the room above, but now her screaming went right off the audible scale. A barrage of French invective, gabbled so fast no words were recognizable.

There was the sound on the stairs of someone going down three at a time, and then the crack of a pistol shot accompanied by a braying laugh that could only be from Dooley.

Reluctantly he swung his legs over the side of the bed, and remembering in time that his companion didn't speak a word of any language he'd ever heard, pointed to his watch, held up five fingers and gestured her to stay there and wait.

As evidence she understood, the Arab girl threw aside the cover and arching her body in the air began to finger herself.

"That's right. Keep it ticking over. Back soon." Failing to find any of his clothes, Revell grabbed a corner of the sheet she'd discarded and wrapping it about himself sarong style, went out onto the landing.

"So what the hell is going on."

There was no answer, but from the flight above came another burst of donkey-like noises. Revell started up, dragging a long white crumpled train in his wake.

"Share the joke then."

Dooley had gathered quite an audience. He sat on the top step with tears of laughter streaming down his face. "It's that jerk Garrett. He chucked a thunderflash under Carrington's bed while he was on the job."

From the room drifted wreaths of gray smoke and anguished sobbing punctuated by vitriolic swearing.

"I thought Carrington was the great unflappable, so why's he chased off after the young prat with a Colt." Scully was minus his shorts, but still had the chef's hat and army boots.

"Carrington might be, but his broad isn't. First thing she did was jump hard enough to almost yank his prick out by the roots, then when the bed burst into flame she shit herself." Dooley dissolved in uncontrollable laughter. He was still laughing and holding his chest when a big naked girl came out and dragged him back to his room.

"Anybody know what kind of state Carrington was in?" Revell made it an open question to the assortment of partially robed figures gradually drifting back to bed.

Scully, with both hands cupped over his privates was edging away with his back to the wall. "I saw him about an hour ago. He was well away, at least a couple of bottles inside him. Garrett's safe enough if he keeps more than ten feet from him."

With that Scully reached an open doorway, and was suddenly gone.

Faintly, from the direction of the lake, came the sound of a shot. Revell pretended not to hear it, and after disentangling his sheet from the stair rails, returned to his own room.

Chapter 9

The dawn revealed long tendrils of mist creeping in off the heath to surround the hotel. Its sickly yellow light did nothing to dispel the chill in the air.

A fire had been lit in a small ground floor lounge, after a long-dead flower arrangement had been removed from the hearth. It lay crushed under the pile of table legs and chair backs that had been broken for fuel.

Garrett sat on the arm of a couch, wincing as their medic dabbed at a cut on his forearm.

"Stop making a fuss." Sampson threw the wad of cotton toward the fire. It missed and slowly frizzled until a spark caused it to be consumed in an instant. "Doesn't even warrant a suture. Come to that, it's hardly worth bothering with a tape, but if you want to try for a purple heart . . . "

"The mad bastard was shooting at me all night. Every time I thought he'd finished, he reloaded." Steering himself, Garrett waited for the wound to be taped. When it didn't hurt he pulled a face anyway, then saw that Sampson hadn't been looking.

"Serves you right." The medic repacked the first-aid kit. "A man doesn't like a strange lady shitting in his bed, no matter what the reason."

"She wasn't a stranger to him." Very gingerly Garrett rolled down his sleeve. He was pleased to see the light-colored bandage showed through the tear in the cloth of his camouflage top. "He'd been bonking with her since two minutes after she'd arrived. I expect he'd have been at her sooner, but it took him that long to run her to his room."

"That's not the point. Doesn't matter how long he's been screwing her, a gentleman doesn't like his companion using his bed as a latrine. Anyway I reckon all the ladies who belong to Frau Lilly's mobile whorehouse are a mite strange. She said as much herself."

"Who? Carrington's broad?"

"No, Frau Lilly. Me and her got to talking last night, sort of an intellectual exchange." Sampson saw the sneer of disbelief in the young PFC's face. "And not that it's any business of yours, but that's all we exchanged. Seems she only involves herself with the administrative side of things."

"Wouldn't catch me wasting time with an old wrinkly."

"You didn't see her, did you. By the time she came in you were already playing mummies and daddies with that puffy faced little tramp with the tattoos."

"She was OK . . . "

"Sure, whatever you fancy, but for your information Frau Lilly is just forty and is she elegant. Used to be a model . . .

"No boobs then." Garrett grinned, pleased to have scored what he saw as an important point.

"Not everyone likes jugs so big they can suffocate you. But tits or no tits I'd rather have spent time with her than be chased around the garden all night by a vengeful drunk with a gun in one hand and a bottle in the other. You know, you're going to get yourself a peculiar reputation in this outfit if you're seen too often being pursued by men wearing nothing but their webbing and bulging ammunition pouches."

Throwing more wood on the fire, Garrett looked for a change of subject. "Who was on guard last night. I don't remember anyone missing out on the party."

"Burke and Old William. Boy, have they got a stack of markers they can call in when they like." Sampson stretched out on a deeply padded Chesterfield, the heels of his boots scuffing the dust from the dark brown leather. "They took it turn and turn about. Old William because he couldn't bear to be associated with all the debauchery going on, and Burke because he's so head over heels for that little Karen he's gone all prim and proper."

Lieutenant Vokes put his head around the door, saw the fire and came in. As he crossed to it he slapped Garrett on his bandaged arm. "He didn't get you then. Pity."

From his pocket he took four small blackened discs, and balancing them on a small ornamental shovel, thrust them into the heart of the spitting fire.

"Some burgers left over from the barbecue. I took them up with me to bed. Sometimes I am hungry in the night. But as it happened I was too busy to think of food."

Noticing the lieutenant had a split lip and a gap between his front teeth, Sampson wondered whether to mention it. Garrett saved him from the dilemma.

"You lost your gold tooth, Lieutenant."

Vokes grinned, and his lip began to bleed. "No I haven't, it's in my pocket." With a splintered table leg he poked the leftovers on the improvised griddle. "One of the girls got over playful. I had my revenge though. When she was going off to sleep I poured something over her lovely little fanny and told her it was superglue. You have never seen panic like it. Took me ages to calm her down and convince her it was only the dregs of a wine glass."

"How many did you have in there? That was only a single room." Garret was awed, but tried not to show it.

"Just the one at first, but later we were joined by a puffy faced little girl with tattoos."

Sampson burst into a laugh, and was still laughing after Garrett had stamped from the room.

Revell stood by his battered old Hummer command car. He couldn't get used to not being surrounded by the usual mass of armor. The general had been taking no chances of their trying to hang onto some of it. Every last APC and armored car had been collected by transporters at first light.

Looking over the men who were assembling nearby, he missed a familiar face and form. "Any one seen Andrea this morning?"

"Going through the empties," Hyde turned from marshalling the company into ranks. "Looking for dregs to drink off a hangover."

The information didn't surprise the major. The girl was becoming more and more of a liability. He would not be able to postpone dealing with her drinking problem for much longer.

There was a lot of squealing and giggling from the direction of the garishly painted transport of the mobile brothel. Frau Lilly was ushering the girls on board. She saw the officer watching and walked over to him.

"There is a little matter to be settled, Major."

While most of the girls were in jeans and sloppy jumpers, or voluminous track suits, Lilly was in a tailored jumpsuit. And instead of the sneakers sported by the others, she wore short high heeled boots.

From a pocket Revell took the cloth wrapped packet whose contents they had jointly gone through the previous evening. As he handed it over he placed on top the thick wad of notes that made up the agreed price.

Ignoring the stack of a paper, Lilly uncovered the small parcel's contents. She prodded through the assorted gem-set items of jewelry. "No offense, Major, but I learned long ago that in business one can never be too careful."

"None taken. It's all there." Despite his reassurance he noticed that she continued her inventory until satisfied.

"Good, I do not have to ask if your men had a good night." She smiled as she surveyed the bleary eyed and haggard soldiers now finally drawn up in two ragged ranks.

For the first time Revell noticed wrinkles at the corners of her eyes that skilfully applied make-up couldn't quite conceal. They did nothing to detract from her looks. Blue-green eyes, perfect teeth and skilfully cut and tinted hair made her outstandingly beautiful.

"At this rate you'll be able to retire soon."

Cramming the payment into a slim white leather purse, she shook her blond hair. "Another five years perhaps. Much of this goes to the girls. I have to pay well or I lose them to the competition, but this is our last time on the road. Tomorrow we move into a proper establishment. It is in Hanover, the City Hotel on Limburgstrasse, do you know it?"

"No, but if it's in the center you'll be closed down within a week."

"I do not think so, Hanover is now virtually an open city. Some of the suburbs have changed hands so many times the children understand Russian as well as they do German."

"Is the overcrowding as bad as ever?" Revell could remember the families of refugees camped in the streets, choking the city center.

"Worse than it has ever been, but where there are people there is always money, or its equivalent."

Revell watched her go back to her transport, the tight fit of her outfit across her bottom revealing that she wore no underwear. As soon as she was aboard the ex-Russian vehicles pulled out, wallowing across the heavily rutted grass.

A strongly built girl waved vigorously from an open roof hatch. Her heavy breasts swung unrestrained inside her tracksuit top.

It was Dooley, Revell noticed, who sheepishly made an answering gesture. He stopped abruptly when he saw he was drawing attention to himself.

"I hope those Russians are a docile bunch." Hyde had been scrutinizing the company. "The state they're in, they'd have problems controlling a church choir."

"They should be, if they're allowing them out of the

cages." Try as he might though, Revell couldn't entirely convince himself of that. He kept recalling the colonel's description of the improvised construction battalion.

Garrett leaned out from the rear radio compartment of the Hummer, nearly strangling himself on the headset cord. "They're almost here, Major."

"They'd have been here by now," Hyde glowered at the PFC. "That's if you'd read the bloody map correctly and passed on the right grid reference when they got lost."

"I wonder what sort of escort they have." Having finally persuaded his Dutch pioneer platoon to form ranks, Vokes had deserted them so as not to be upset by their constantly changing places to discuss with friends the events of the night.

"We'll know in a few minutes. Probably got some staff officer from Division tagging along, to make sure we don't goof off. That's why I've had the men turn out, for the sake of appearances." Revell cast a pained look over his command. "Not so sure it's a good idea any more though. Sergeant Hyde!"

"Sir."

"Do something with them, will you. I know they feel awful, but there's no need for them to look it as well. And Lieutenant Vokes . . ."

In anticipation of what was coming, Vokes gave a resigned shrug.

" . . . From here it looks as if your men are involved in some bizarre slow motion dance. If you can't get them to stand up straight, at least see if you can get them to stand still."

"They're real close now, Major." Garrett was more careful this time, and only managed to unplug himself from the set. "Reception is brilliant."

"Really? Well I must say I'm hardly surprised, seeing as they're driving in through the gate at this moment."

"No wonder they're three hours late. Looks like they had a bit of an adventure on the way." Hyde watched a very battered Unimog light truck grind its way toward them, its stately ten-mile-an-hour rate of progress being dictated by severely buckled front wheels.

The panelwork of the cab showed further evidence of a hard collision, as did the starred windshield and ripped fabric roof. As it crabbed an erratic course along the drive the Unimog scuffed strange patterns on the gravel. Into view behind it came a procession of equally decrepit ex-civilian single deck buses.

The truck came to a halt beside the Hummer with a screech of brakes more in keeping with an emergency stop from ninety. After what sounded like several hard kicks the driver's door creaked open and an elderly and overweight master sergeant alighted, easing his bulk with care over the jagged remains of the fender. He beat dust from his blood speckled camouflage jacket before looking about him.

"Is there a medic hereabouts?"

The sergeant dabbed at his swollen nose with a red-stained handkerchief.

"You run into trouble?" Revell scanned the now halted column. Faces filled every window of the convoy. Apart from the truck there were only the buses. "And where the hell are the escort?"

"Shit, I'll say I ran into trouble. Some damned crappy refugees, they were all over the road. Wish I'd creamed a few of them, instead of taking to the hill and whacking into the side of a fucking church. Ain't there a medic here? This keeps up, I'm going to bleed to death."

"I asked where the escort had got to." Revell knew that his tone clearly conveyed his growing anger, but the master sergeant appeared not to notice.

"Oh heck Major, there's no escort, excepting for me and my drivers." He waved vaguely in the direction of the buses. "We had a handful or so with us for a while but they must have missed a turn, or stopped for a leak maybe . . . anyway, haven't seen them for a couple of hours or more. Maybe five, I guess. Don't matter though. These here Ruskies are like pussycats. If you'll just sign, I'll find your medic then I'll be getting back. I got a date for tonight."

Not accepting the clipboard and greasy pen held out toward him, Revell started toward the new arrivals. "I like to see what I'm signing for, I want a roll call."

"Hell, you don't want to bother with all that fuss, Major. It's real straightforward. I deliver three hundred and fifty-seven Reds. Or maybe they ought to be called pinks now, heh?" Seeing his little joke wasn't well-received, the sergeant went on. "I deliver, you sign. See, everybody is happy and I make my date on time. If we start messing about with roll calls and the like we could be here all day."

"A roll call, now."

"Now Major, I hope you won't mind me saying this . . ."

"I probably will, so you'd better not."

For the first time, the sergeant appeared to be getting a glimmering of an understanding that the officer was less than happy with something.

"OK Major, OK, we do it by the book. But maybe it

wouldn't hurt if we take a sort of shortcut, just to speed things up a little. See, there's seven buses, fifty Reds on each one, excepting the last. That's got fifty-seven. So we do a swift head count on the tail-end Charlie and that's . . ."

"I see only six."

"Hate to say it, but you're wrong Major, it's seven . . ."

The sergeant did a double take and a sickly grin spread across his fleshy face. "Aw crap. Fucking crap. Well, I expect it'll be along in a while. Look Major, can I have a word?"

When Revell wouldn't be drawn aside, the sergeant leaned close to him and lowered his voice to a confidential whisper.

"I'm just sort of doing a favor for my captain; you know how it is, sure you do. He was on to this sure thing, a real hot date, and I figured if I did this favor for him then I'd be OK for a few in return. Happens all the time." He looked keenly into the officer's face, trying to read his mood, and didn't like what he saw.

"Right, Major, you think I've goofed up. So maybe everything ain't quite kosher, but in the Zone who cares what happens to fifty . . . "

"Fifty-seven."

" . . . Sure, fifty-seven Reds. Shit, we've got a half million behind wire and there's loads more who've deserted and are just wandering about. Can't we sort of overlook the discrepancy this time? You know I should have been retired years ago. It's not my fault I'm still in this stinking war, I . . ."

"It sounds like you and your captain are a good pair." Revell beckoned Sergeant Hyde. "I want them out of the transport and lined up in fives. Keep a good guard on them."

"We could use the tennis courts. The wire's still standing around them."

"Good idea. And we'll have that lot down for checking as well." Revell pointed to the mountain of cases and bags loosely secured and partially sheeted on the roof of each bus.

"Is there anything I can do, Major?" The convoy commander ran his finger around the inside of his collar to loosen it. Blood was again dripping from his burst nose but he ignored it and instead wiped away with the back of his hand the perspiration that was running down the side of his face.

"You're already doing it. And you'll be sweating a lot more blood by the time I'm finished."

Chapter 10

"The fifty-seven in the missing bus you know about." Hyde consulted his lists. "There are another thirty unaccounted for from those who did arrive. That gives us two hundred and sixty-eight milling about on the hard court."

"Should be two hundred and seventy, shouldn't it?" Revell watched the Russians listlessly moving about the makeshift compound.

"There are two stiffs on board the second bus. Seems the MPs who broke up the fights didn't want the bother of hauling them off and sorting out the attendant paperwork."

"And that master sergeant called them pussycats. What happened to the other thirty?"

"I've had a chat with the drivers. Seems our fat friend accepted a bribe to make regular stops during the night for them to get off and have a leak. The Ruskies were allowed off all at once and no guard kept or recount made when they got back in, and no one has any clue as to when the seventh coach went astray."

"Well at least that all indicates that those we still

have, if they haven't made a break for it by now, then they're not going to at all." Revell prodded the pile of contraband at his feet with the barrel of his assault shotgun. "Mind you, that doesn't mean we're not going to get any hassle from them. Was this all found among their baggage?"

Bending down he picked up a civilian shotgun that had been shortened by the removal of most of the stock and half the twin over and under barrels. He broke it to check it had been unloaded, then tossed it back on the substantial heap.

"We spotted some of them carrying the stuff, but most of it came from their luggage. There are twenty-six pistols or cut down rifles, forty-two grenades of every type, five pounds of plastic explosive and three detonators." Hyde scanned his list. "Also four hatchets, eight hammers . . . didn't bother to count the knives. Would have been quicker to weigh them."

"Dump it all in the lake, the whole lot. Pity we can't do the same with the recent owners." Among the collection Revell spotted an ornate Nazi dagger of World War Two vintage. Doubtless it had been looted from some abandoned property. It was likely the civvy shotgun came from a similar source. "These Reds may no longer be on the Warpac side, but I've got my doubt that they're on ours either."

Penned within the confines of the high mesh fences, the Russians strolled or lounged on the ground wrapped in soiled greatcoats. They appeared to be completely apathetic as to their surroundings, taking no interest in anything. There was little conversation among them, not even when their cases and bags had been checked in their full view. No concern, curiosity or resentment was displayed when the finds began to be made, not even when the haul was removed for disposal.

The only spark of animation came when Sampson and one of the pioneers appeared with buckets of water. Then there was a mad scramble for the gate where it was ladled out. It had taken several shots fired into the air to restore any semblance of order.

A thorough search of the transport uncovered another twelve guns and several hundred rounds of assorted ammunition, plus many more edged weapons. Revell was reluctant to, but it was beginning to look as if they would have to bodysearch every one of their prisoners. That was the conclusion he was reaching when Lieutenant Vokes brought one of the Russians to him.

"This one speaks English, after a fashion, Major. He says he wants to . . ."

"To talk to the major, yes. That is what I am asking."

"Make it quick." Despite himself, Revell couldn't help smiling. The man before him looked like a cartoon composite of the typical Russian.

He stood about five foot nine, but was so broad in the chest and across the shoulders that he looked squat. A short bull neck was topped by a heavy jowled slab of a face. His eyes were dark and narrow, made to look the more so by a broad forehead framed by a severe fringe of jet black hair.

All in all the Russian reminded Revell of a younger version of Brezhnev.

Moving ponderously to attention, the Russian made as if to salute, but after his hand jerked twice in indecision he didn't.

"Grigori Vladimirovich Galinski at your service, Major. Late sergeant in the 445th Company of the Commandants Service, attached to the 75th Infantry regiment, 3rd Shock Army."

"I'm surprised you are still alive. Do your present companions not know you were with the military police?"

"To survive, one sometimes has to resort to subterfuge, Major. When I crossed the Zone to defect I assumed the identity of a . . . a friend, who unfortunately died on the journey. I tell you this so that you can be assured of my good faith."

"You think I need reassuring?" Revell would have dismissed the man, but something made him hesitate. Perhaps he could be useful.

"By telling you this, I place myself in your hands, Major. Perhaps by so doing I might gain trust that would otherwise take a long time to establish."

"Do you have any influence among this rabble?" Indicating the inmates of the compound, Revell saw that they had resumed their apathetic bahavior now the distribution of the water ration was over.

The Russian thumped himself on the chest, raising a puff of dust. "They know that I am a strong man, a tough boss." He made the familiar Russian gesture of a clenched fist. "A powerful boss is always respected in my country."

"Like Stalin." Overcoming his distaste of the prisoner, Revell realized he might be able to use him. "We've wasted too much time here already. I want all the weapons this mob of yours is carrying."

"Everything?"

Revell knew he was expecting too much if he thought

he could net every knife among them, without resorting to a strip search. That would waste the best part of a half day.

"Firearms, grenades, explosives and ammunition. When they come out of there in fifteen minutes I want to see it all in a pile in the middle of the court. Just to be on the safe side my men will do random checks. If we find anything in that list, then there'll be no food issue today."

That is a very fair arrangement, Major, very fair. I am sure I can get them to go along with it. If there is anything else I can do?"

"I'll let you know." And he would! Revell had to give the man a high mark for initiative, even if it was prompted by self interest. Among the Russian people a display of initiative was considered dangerous, a trait to be stamped on ruthlessly. So rarely was it ever practiced that they didn't even have a word for it in their language. "By what name are you known, if I need you again?"

"It is fortunate, Major, that my late comrade and I shared the same first name. A call for Grigori will soon find me."

Revell didn't doubt that. The man was obviously an operator. He wondered how long it would be before, perhaps, he had to stamp on him.

"You're ready then?"

The convoy sergeant had been dogging Revell's footsteps, and hovering about him through all the preparations for departure. All of that time he had been carrying the clipboard with the unsigned receipt.

Whichever way he turned Revell found himself faced by it, and a proffered pen, like a supplicant's petition.

On top of the buses the new guards had finally settled in among nests of rearranged luggage. Those of the combat company and the pioneers who were to travel in the trucks and Hummers were already boarding.

Revell took a last look around to check that preparations were complete, then finally accepted the offered board. Crossing through the typed figures at the bottom of the torn and creased greasy paper, he wrote in the actual number he'd received live. Signing it and handing it back, he watched the master sergeant's expression as he read the alteration. He was far from happy.

"Ah hell, Major. There ain't something you could add, just to sort of soften it a little, is there? You know, about the escort going astray, maybe something on those lines."

"You can explain that for yourself when you get back. Next time leave your captain to do his own dirty work. And if I were you I'd get those wheels changed on your transport. If the military police spot you motoring like that, they can have you on a sabotage rap. You've got enough problems as it is."

Exhaust smoke plumed above the lengthening column parked on the drive, as the company's transports were jockeyed into place between each of the buses.

The perimeter of the grounds was lined with refugees. Having watched with greedy eyes every stage of the preparations for the move, they now became bolder and began to filter hesitantly toward the abandoned building. Gradually the pace of the cautious infiltration increased as they weren't challenged. Inevitably they began to converge on the kitchen area, and just as inevitably scuffles and fights began to occur.

As he ducked into his Hummer, Revell took a last look at the imposing building. In an hour or two it would be a shell, stripped of everything movable. It was a wonder it had escaped such depredations for so long. For a while yet it might have remained intact, if the presence of the combat company had not drawn attention to it.

Perhaps a few of the refugees would settle there for a while, until every last sliver of furniture and fittings had been consumed by the cooking fires. But it would not be for long. Disease was constantly thinning the numbers of civilians in the Zone, despite the constant replenishment caused by the frequent expansion of its area, as a consequence of fresh battles or advances. Certainly the old hotel would be abandoned the moment the truce ended. A conspicuous building was a dangerous place to be while there was fighting.

That it had escaped serious damage for such a length of time made it all the more likely that its turn for violent demolition would be soon.

For those pathetic displaced persons now struggling over scraps, the only comparative safety would be that offered by the larger refugee camps. There, overcrowding and the total breakdown of any semblance of law made life only marginally better. The Red Cross and the other relief agencies could do little faced with the vast numbers involved.

Taking his place in the front passenger seat, Revell saw that Andrea was already behind the wheel. Her foot tapped out an impatient series of loud revs from the gas pedal. Her action betrayed at least one fresh hole in the much patched muffler.

She looked like she'd been on a three day binge. Her hair was matted and her eyes red-rimmed and bloodshot. From the slack fit of her battledress Revell figured that she was also losing weight. Where it had been tight over her chest and hips, its folds now concealed her shape. As yet her drinking hadn't affected her fighting capabilities, but then he'd not put her in a position where she'd been really tested. At the rate she was going though, it would not be long before he had to do something about her. Once, because of how he'd felt about her, she would've had special treatment. Not any more.

"We're all set. Give them a blast." Cradling his assault shotgun, Revell wished his hands were free so that he could stuff his fingers in his ears.

Andrea kept her hand down hard on the air-horn. The blare of the klaxon seemed to make his skull vibrate.

"That'll do. I think they got the message." Revell estimated they had a three hour journey. With Garrett occupied on his radio watch in the rear compartment and with this silent and unsmiling driver, it was going to seem a lot longer.

Chapter 11

"Scorched earth. With a vengeance."

Revell had to agree with Sergeant Hyde. It certainly looked as if those were the tactics that had been employed by the Warpac unit that pulled back from the area.

On his map Revell had it marked as an area of extensive demolitions. That told only a fraction of the story. The road here ran through thick woodland and what had once been a Russian encampment. There was little left by which to identify it as such.

What had been a complex of deep bunkers, skilfully linked by an extensive network of trenches and weapon pits was now a wasteland. Powerful explosions had caved in whole sections, and what had been missed by them showed ample evidence of having been churned and bulldozed. Fire had completed the work of destruction and the air still reeked with the distinctive smell of flame-thrower fuel and phosphorus residue.

Even a motorcycle and sidecar, presumably beyond repair and not worthy of salvage, had been crushed into the soft loam, like a modern-day fossil.

Masses of tall pines and firs had been toppled and now formed an impenetrable entwined and splintered mass across the road.

"It looks like they blasted everything, then ran across the whole lot with a squadron of tanks." Revell pushed the flattened motorcycle with the toe of his boot. It didn't yield. "They didn't mean to leave anything for us, did they? I thought when we drove over the rest of our section our pet Russians were in for an easy time. I see now that they're not." He turned to Lieutenant Vokes. "You're the expert in this sort of work. Where do we start?"

Vokes surveyed the torn and heavily cratered road. In places it was bared to a depth of several feet where spoil from detonations close alongside had rained down. He had tried counting the trees that lay across it, but had given up when he reached sixty, with at least as many more still to go.

"I think the orders are that we have ten days to open up twenty kilometers?" He looked to the major for an answering nod of confirmation. Another glance at the road and he sucked in air through the gap in his teeth. "This section is by far the worst. I would think it would absorb seventy-five percent of our work force for the whole of that period. We are lucky it is virtually in the middle. I would suggest we camp and concentrate our effort here. The other road blocks, and that collapsed culvert, we can send working parties out to deal with each day, as they are required. It is a shame we do not have even one power shovel, or dump truck."

"Haven't, and aren't likely to get. I'll put in a request all the same." Revell made a note on a message pad. "A few chain saws wouldn't go amiss either."

A blurred outline of the sun was sitting on the western horizon and among the trees the shadows had lengthened to infinity. As they walked back to where the column stood it became rapidly darker. Here, the trees still stood, crowding out the light.

There might be a truce in force but Revell could take no chances. The previous night had been a rare opportunity to relax in the Zone. Tonight they were right on the edge of the temporary truce strip. A bare six kilometers away was the Warpac side. If anything went wrong, they would be the very first to know about it. A few minutes or even seconds' warning might be enough to save some of their lives.

The guards that were already posted had a dual function though. They were positioned as much to watch that no one bolted into the trees, or appeared out of them.

"So they stay on the buses for tonight?" From the rear of the long file of vehicles Hyde heard the clatter of Scully preparing the evening meal. It would be their first, and only, hot meal of the day. The same would be served up for all of them, NATO troops and Warpac prisoner battalion alike.

"It'll be simpler that way. At first light we'll find a suitable clearing and keep a few of them back to erect a perimeter fence and put up the tents."

"They'll be better off than us."

Revell knew what Hyde meant, and knew it would rankle with the men. For the Russians it would be the comparative space and warmth of the buses. No guard duty for them, stumbling about in the dark, hearing and seeing things that weren't there as fatigue played tricks with eyes.

At least there appeared to be no mines, but in the major's mind that constituted something of an enigma. Even in its demolished state it was evident that the unit that had previously occupied the site had been able to call on lavish field engineer support. To have completed such extensive work would have called for a prodigious effort, of a sort not usually available to a formation probably not much above battalion strength.

And yet there were no mines. Hardly any barbed or razor wire either. Without those it was tempting to think the position had been prepared in advance of requirement, needing only those additions to activate it. But that was obviously not the case. Latrine trenches showed it had been occupied, and for some time.

Even more than the absence of mines, it was the lack of wire that puzzled Revell. He could recall several occasions when he had traveled through a landscape scraped clean by nuclear air-bursts. Every building was pulverized to the last brick, trees and telegraph poles burnt to below ground level. In so surreal a place the wisps of smoke from charring stumps had made it resemble an abandoned camp ground. And yet there had been the wire, partially buried or tumbled into giant rust and flame streaked concertinas, it was still there. Mines might be lifted for re-use, but wire?

Such a vast expenditure of effort, for what? An extravagant, almost profligate expenditure of man and machine hours to defend an insignificant unit in a quiet sector. Perhaps the answer would become clear in the morning. Time enough to puzzle over it then. At least he wouldn't be waking up with a hangover again, and the nagging worry as to what he might have caught this time.

"Dooley wants a word with you, Major."

"Can't it wait until the morning, Sergeant Hyde. And what's come over him that suddenly he should decide to do things the correct way. Usually he simply saunters over and starts a conversation."

"I've no idea. He's been acting funny all evening."

"In what way?"

"He's gone quiet."

"I see what you mean. Well, send him over. Let's see what it's all about."

So what would it be this time? Since he'd first had him under his command, Revell had seen their anti-tank expert materialize a hundred or more ailments or excuses. All were imagined and all were intended to get him off some detail he didn't fancy. He should have asked his sergeant what guard duty Dooley had drawn. That might have offered an explanation. But Dooley going quiet . . . that was a new one.

"Permission to speak, sir."

The "sir," and the salute which accompanied it were definitely unique phenomena. It put Revell on his guard immediately. With the exception of Old William, who never offered more than a nod of recognition to officers, Dooley was probably the least military of any of his men.

"I'm listening."

"It's a rather personal matter, sir."

Revell looked about. They were fifty meters from the closest vehicle, as much again from the nearest sentry. "We're as alone as we'll ever be."

Despite that reassurance Dooley still made his own check of the surrounding gloom. "I'd like to apply for leave, sir. On compassionate grounds."

That was more like it. They were now on familiar territory. It was a ploy he recognized, and prepared to meet it. In the last twelve months Dooley had alleged the death of all his relatives down to second cousins, in similar attempts. Whatever his reason, it wouldn't take a moment to knock down. They'd had no mail for a month so he wouldn't be easily able to pluck any long lost uncle who languished on the threshold of death.

"Go on."

"I want to get married."

All of Revell's stock replies went out the window.

"Why?" Even as he said it he realized it was a stupid damned thing to ask, but in the shock of the moment it was all he could come up with.

"I'm in love, sir."

"Known the young lady long?" Suspicion lurked in Revell's mind. "It is a young lady, is it? Not one of the, shall we say, more mature females I've seen you with."

"She's about twenty . . . twenty-five . . . well, about that, sir."

Understanding began to dawn on the major. "So how long have you known this young lady of twenty or possibly twenty-five, with whom you are so in love."

"Since about this time yesterday, Major."

"And her name?"

This time Dooley didn't blurt out his response. He shifted from one foot to the other, looking at the ground.

"Actually . . . well we didn't . . . that is, we didn't get down to exchanging names."

"A case of actions speaking louder than words, I take it. You're not thinking of chasing off after her, are you?"

"You know me better than that, Major. Request denied then, is it, sir?"

It would have been easy for Revell to dismiss the matter as a joke, but for all he knew Dooley could be quite serious, if not very practical. Certainly stranger things had happened to others in the combat company. Burke's transformation, for instance.

The eldest, until Vokes's pioneers had joined them and brought Old William along, a real old soldier and barrack room lawyer, he had changed overnight when Karen Hirsh had come on the scene. The chubby little nurse, barely out of her teens, had really got to him.

And there was Libby, one of their most reliable men. He'd deserted, gone back into the Zone to look for his Helga.

"I think you've got to get things on a more realistic footing first, don't you? We'll be through here in a couple of weeks. Look her up then. At least that'll give you a chance to get better acquainted, maybe find out her name."

Dooley grinned, and all thought of saluting forgotten, wandered off wearing a thoughtful but satisfied expression.

Maybe, Revell thought, he should have squashed the idea flat, but what the hell. For all his faults, Dooley was a good infantryman. If he needed a dream to keep him going, and it was more realistic than his vague plans to become a roving toy-boy in Miami, who was he to shatter it.

In a way he could even envy him. All Revell had got out of the previous night was the fulfillment of a physical needs. His girl had been good in bed, too good perhaps, if the ache in his back and the soreness of his penis was anything to go by. Yes, let Dooley keep his dream. Most likely it would only last until the next hooker came along, or until his forever scheming brain was again immersed in plans of servicing every rich widow and generous divorcee in Florida.

Still, he'd rather his men brooded over matters of that sort than dwell too much on their chances of coming through the war alive, and in one piece. Not that in all truth there was the slightest possibility of any of them managing that miracle.

As he made his way to his Hummer, and an uncomfortable night on the ground beside it, he thought of Thorne. His future was a standard issue coffin in a military cemetery that stretched as far as the horizon. It was not enough that his remains were slashed and mutilated beyond recognition. A final indignity would be his interment in a plot especially reserved for contaminated corpses.

Strange to worry about spreading poison to a plot only six by six by two, when millions of acres of Europe were already contaminated by chemicals and bacteria and massive doses of radiation.

Even when you were dead the Zone still clung to you, keeping you an outcast, forcing you to remain a part of it.

Revell gave himself a mental shake. He was thinking too much, and about the wrong things. Shouting aboard one of the buses drew his mind away, and for once he welcomed the diversion.

Chapter 12

"At this rate we'll be able to take back those that are left alive in just the one bus." Revell scowled at the three bodies the dawn roll-call had produced. "Will somebody close their eyes."

Sampson bent down to do it.

"And while you're at it, check those wounds. What caused them, and how long ago?" Pacing up and down in front of the shuffling Russians, Revell noticed that all avoided catching his eye. They were an ugly and disreputable looking crowd to begin with. The furtive behavior did nothing to improve his opinion of them. It was obviously assumed, as on turning around, he would sometimes catch one slyly grinning at the corpses, or nudging his companion in the ranks and offering a whispered comment. The instant they realized they were observed down would come the attitude of shifty subservience, like a veil across their face.

While Sampson made a quick inspection of the bodies, Scully went through their pockets. Most were already pulled inside out and he found only a single rifle round that had slipped through a hole in a coat lining.

"Two of them got it real quick, Major." Sampson looked up at the officer as he wriggled fingers through a small tear in the chest panel of a shirt." The one on the end, with the red beard, I reckon he bled to death. Must have taken a couple of hours. He's still warm, so if it all happened about the same time then, maybe around 3 A.M. would be a pretty accurate guess."

At the back of the fidgeting Russians Revell identified a familiar figure, trying to make itself inconspicuous and drawing attention to itself by so doing.

"Grigori, out here."

There was a ripple of movement and the ranks parted to let him through. "Is there something you are wanting, Major?"

He held a woolen cap in his big rough hands, and was slowly wringing it until threads started to part. Revell hadn't seen him with it the previous day, and it appeared that whatever the weather the Russians wore all their clothing, presumably to stop it from being stolen. "You were on that bus. I know there is no point in asking who did this, but I'd like to know why."

Grigori turned his palms forward and spread his arms in a gesture of ignorance. "I was asleep, Major. I woke when the first fight happened in the late evening, when you yourself came in, but after that . . . I sleep very heavily . . . "

"I want to know what happened."

"You must appreciate my position, Major. You will see the others appear to be listening, very attentively. I do not think any of them understand English, but there are some who keep such things to themselves, if you understand me." He lowered his voice and took a step nearer the officer. "Perhaps if you would escort me a little distance away, at gun point. A push or two would also look well. For the sake of appearances?"

Unslinging his shotgun, the pushes Revell administered with the butt of it were more than just for appearances. "That's far enough, now unless you're also afraid they can lip read as well, let's have it."

"You understand I had no part in it . . ."

"I understand you'd not tell me if you were. Get on with it."

"There has been bad blood, for some days. The three men who died . . . Yes, good, keep the gun leveled at me, Major, but with the safety on?"

"I'm happy with it like this."

"As you wish." Grigori used the cap to wipe his forehead. "It is going to be a hot day." He saw the tip of the 12 bore barrel elevate a fraction, toward his stomach. "The three men who died had been stealing tobacco."

"So you all ganged up on them." Revell had been expecting something of the sort.

"Oh no, Major. I assure you I was asleep, and so were many of the others, and the three who are laid over there. I explain. They had not been stealing from everyone, they had only been taking it from thieves who had stolen it from everyone."

"So the thieves got their own back. You know who the thieves are?" Revell got precisely the answer he anticipated.

"Sometimes one suspects, but they are so clever, one can never be sure. After all, if a man is known to be a thief then he is allowed few opportunities."

Revell gestured with the shotgun. "Get back with the others. I'm going to work you so hard that by tonight you'll all sleep."

"Will you not need supervisors, Major? I can . . ." Grigori saw the expression on the American's face and didn't finish the sentence.

The bodies were buried without ceremony in a common grave, actually a partially collapsed dug-out. A few blows with a pick axe brought the remains of the roof down.

The earth had barely settled before working parties under Sergeant Hyde and Lieutenant Vokes departed, to tackle the lighter damage of other sections of the road.

Those remaining under Revell's command he split into two equal groups. One he set to erect the tents and perimeter fence of their own compound: the other to begin the daunting task of clearing and repairing the road through the enemy position.

For all the rough and burly appearance the Russians presented, the major quickly discovered them to be soft. They tired quickly. In the case of some it was definitely an act. Concentrating the worst of the goldbrickers into a platoon bossed by Andrea and Clarence brought about a marked improvement.

Within an hour it was obvious that manpower alone would not be sufficient for the task of clearing the trees. An attempt was made to clear a particularly dense tangle of fallen timber using fire. After piling every combustible fragment that could be found around the trunks, diesel fuel was poured over and a phosphorus grenade used to ignite the stack.

It roared into flame, giving off walls of heat that

drove them well back. Flaring red and yellow tongues would frequently lick out toward the forest, threatening to spread the blaze.

After an hour the brushwood had been reduced to a low mound of gray ash. The waves of fierce heat it radiated meant it had to be smothered with dirt before it could be approached. Above it, although heavily charred, the tree trunks remained intact. Only one had burned through to the point where it had begun to sag under its own weight.

When Revell got through to Divisional HQ on the radio with a request for explosives to speed the work he was turned down flat.

"I guess we're out of favor at the moment." He handed the headset back to Garrett, who managed to drop it.

"Back to the dark ages then." Corporal Carrington threw a large pine cone at a Russian who had stopped work to pick his nose in leisurely fashion.

The missile struck him between the shoulder blades and he instantly resumed work with his shovel.

"Near enough." Revell was beginning to feel more than a little discouraged. "We've got the winch on the Hummer, but from now on most of it is going to be down to brute force and ignorance."

"Where do we start?"

"Give the axes to the best workers. Pair them up so that as one tires the other can take it over. For what's left of today we'll concentrate on trimming side branches so that we can get nice clean pulls."

"And the rest of them?" Carrington hefted another cone, ready for further targets.

"Put them on getting the debris off the road. There's

tons of the stuff. Have them dump it and compact it where the curb has disintegrated."

Revell watched the temporary bustle the change of instruction prompted. It was of even shorter duration than he'd anticipated. Despite careful organization, in many cases meaning that individual Russians were allocated specific jobs, the work still seemed to go ahead with an ant hill-like confusion.

While some shovelled at the mounds of soil, others carried the spoil they dislodged to places where fill was needed. There others would spread and compact it. Progress appeared pathetically slow. The more so when Revell calculated that what was going to take more than three hundred men above a week, could be done by a JCB or Cat in a day.

The party working the hardest was definitely that where Andrea was an overseer. She constantly prowled the fringes of the area being worked, finger on the trigger of her M16. Aided by a few basic words of Russian and many threatening looks and gestures she spurred the group to ever greater effort.

Men twice her size would break into a stumbling run when she shouted. They'd hurl their loads into a crater and double back for more.

Every time he passed him, Revell saw Grigori put on an act of frenetic activity, all the while bellowing encouragement to others to exert themselves. He would then look up at the officer, as if noticing his presence for the first time, wipe imagined sweat from his face with his cap and nod confidentially.

Revell often had to look away as he attempted to keep a straight face. Though he passed him over a score of times, not once did Grigori miss his cue.

By late afternoon the speed of work had slowed to a snail's pace. The men paused frequently to spit on their palms to ease the sting of broken blisters.

At seventeen hundred Revell called a halt, and radioed for the other two groups to return. He found both were ready to come back. Their men were in similar condition, unfit to work any longer.

It did not add up to an auspicious start. During the journey on the previous day Revell had entertained vague thoughts of blitzing through the work and finding something, anything, to do with the remaining time. On current performance it looked like they'd be hard pressed to complete the task if the truce should last three weeks.

On his return Vokes reported that he only needed two more days. Hyde's estimate of four to five days to fill a series of huge craters was not so comforting, but it did mean the whole battalion would be on hand for a final effort to complete work within the allotted timescale.

As the laborers stacked their implements and made their way to where Scully was dishing out stew, many made much play of limping. Others walked bent almost double with hands clutching their backs.

Watching, Revell knew that a few cases would be quite genuine. Several men had taken cracking blows on their feet or shins from carelessly wielded picks or shovels. But there had fortunately been no resulting broken bones and the worst Sampson had dealt with had been cuts and bruises.

Among the malingerers few displayed the sheer artistry of Grigori. Walking stiffly erect, his expression contrived to give the impression of a man who was suffering greatly, but trying heroically not to show it. If he was disappointed at his ploy not succeeding, he didn't reveal it in any way.

"Are we sure that these men deserted the Warpac armies in order to help the NATO side?" Vokes watched the shuffling rabble speed up as it caught the smell of the food. "If these are typical of their sort then I am forced to believe the KGB planted them on us to slow our war effort."

A roll call went surprisingly easily, with only three recounts required to reach the correct total. That done, they were herded into their compound. Dooley tried to march them in, but swiftly gave it up as a bad job. He left it to Andrea, who stalked after them like an aggressive sheep dog. The last to enter were pushing hard on the heels of those ahead.

Their slight stock of razor wire meant that only a few strands could be stretched out to surround the compound area. Knowing that was all they could manage, Revell had ensured that the site was level and thoroughly cleared of undergrowth. It had also been kept as compact as possible and the straight sides made the duty of patrolling the perimeter that much easier.

He would have preferred more space between the thirty bell tents, but the extent of the clearing did not permit it. There would be little that could be done to prevent movement within the camp. A couple of lights, powered off a recharging generator, were positioned at opposite corners. They would have the effect of making the center of the area all the darker. That would have to be a secondary consideration.

There would be no moon, but the major was reasonably confident with the prisoners in their exhausted state, they would be unlikely to create problems during the short summer night. If matters got out of control there would be casualties on both sides of the wire.

A breeze ruffled the tops of the trees. Revell looked up. The sky was still light, with the few wisps of clouds showing as red scars as the sinking sun caught them. It was only a couple of days since the fighting had ceased. He was amazed at the difference it already made to the atmosphere. Now the only smoke he could smell was the faint aroma of pine ash. Visibility had improved markedly, and every breath he took seemed the fresher for it.

"Lieutenant Vokes!"

The Dutchman appeared, still in the act of consuming his third helping of stew.

"Take over, will you. I'm going to scout around. There's a path of sorts, heads to the south. I want to see if it leads to a dump."

"You should take an escort, Major. And if you find a dump, watch out for booby-traps. I have lost men that way."

Replacing the buckshot round in his shotgun for a cartridge filled with flechettes, Revell nodded agreement. It was Ripper his gaze lit on first. It wasn't the best choice he could have made but it was the quickest. Within a couple of minutes he was wondering if it would have been better to take his time and pick some one else instead.

"Sure nice of you to invite me along, Major. Sergeant Hyde had me cramped up, all alone, on radio watch in the Land Rover all day. I feel like the original dead-end kid. Like I told the sarge . . ."

Revell let him rattle on, taking little notice. Not that telling him to shut up would have made any lasting difference. He'd only start up again with a few minutes. If indeed he could hold out that long. Burke described the young PFC as having verbal diarrhea. It was apt.

Most of them had got used to him, but the non-stop chatter, the never ending stream of peculiar stories about his weird family back home, it got to you occasionally. That was very likely why Hyde had set him in such an isolated post all day.

To reach the beaten track Revell had spotted they'd have to skirt the scene of utter devastation that was all that was left of the Warpac position.

Although well trodden where it wound beneath the trees, the path was only wide enough for one. Now Revell reconsidered the merits of his choice of companion. Ripper had the eyes of a hawk. If the route had been mined he'd spot it in good time.

At a cautious but steady pace they followed the track. No others diverged from it. Several times, at irregular intervals they passed discarded vodka bottles. Most were broken, many were cloudy with age.

In their condition, Revell saw further evidence that this was not some fall-back position. Obviously the enemy had been in occupation for a lengthy period.

The path climbed steadily, but they didn't have to exert themselves. Now and again there were unidentifiable scraps of rag caught on low branches, or trampled into the ground.

After a half kilometer Revell felt sure that it would only lead to some outpost situated on high ground, perhaps with a view of the road. He could imagine the troops of the relief detail swigging from the bottles as soon as they were out of sight of their officers and NCOs.

The track reached its highest point, but there was no machine gun nest or observation post. Down a steep slope lay a small lightly wooded valley. A stream ran through the center of it.

Of all the sights that in a moment of idle speculation, Revell might have thought he'd see, this was by far the least expected.

Filling the floor of the valley was another scene of total destruction, but a very different one from that they had recently left.

Chapter 13

The refugee camp had been put to the torch. A few shelters had escaped and they stood forlornly amid the mass of charred wreckage.

"It's the first one I've ever seen with defenses like that." As they walked nearer, Ripper could see the ribbons of rusted razor wire roughly fastened to crude stakes. At regular intervals stood the half burned stumps of watch towers.

Revell too had been noting the unusual features of the place. Experience led him to estimate that it had once held two and a half thousand displaced people. That was twice the number the casual observer might have hazarded, but he was familiar with the lean-to building techniques the refugees used. The method led to a lot of people packing into a surprisingly compact area.

They passed through an opening, stepping across a toppled, strongly built gate. A few curls of smoke still rose from the ruins.

"Those towers wouldn't give them much of a warning." From the remains of one close at hand Revell made a calculated guess at the height it had stood. "But it would give someone a good view of the camp."

"Like a Red with a machine gun." Ripper plucked a Cindy doll from the remains of a hut. Half the face had burnt away and the little dress had crisped to a brittle shroud.

"So now we know how the Russians could put so many man hours into the defense positions by the road." Walking across the wreckage, Revell was at least glad to see no evidence of bodies. "Looks like they took their slave laborers with them."

"At least they're still alive then." Scuffing his foot through a pile of cinders Ripper uncovered smoldering fragments of thick cardboard. He placed the disfigured doll on top of the smoldering ashes. Flame broke out about it, and it shrivelled to nothing. The air filled with black specks of plastic as the miniature pyre completed the immolation.

On the far side of the camp, out beyond the wire, was a small marked off area containing a sprinkling of crude crosses, and headstones made from scraps of chipboard.

It was not something Revell could regard as sinister. The death rate among refugees was high, from many causes, the majority natural. The numbers represented in that pathetic graveyard were in no way exceptional.

They turned to leave, stepping over the wire where it sagged after posts had burned away. A movement caught Revell's attention.

On a broad freshly turned tract of the valley floor, two dogs were scratching and growling at the ground. He'd noticed the bare earth on the way down, but had dismissed it as simply a vegetable patch. Now the animals' actions drew it to his attention.

Even as the hounds turned toward them he was unslinging the shotgun. Foam flecking the sides of their mouths, tongues lolling over bared teeth, the dogs bounded toward them.

The storm of steel darts caught them when they were still thirty meters away. Deforming into hooks as they penetrated, the flechettes ripped them open and sent them bounding and twisting into the air. The one that was still alive when they crashed back to the ground, Ripper dispatched with a single round through the tormented creature's skull.

"Why would a couple of brutes like them be interested in grubbing up carrots?" Ripper followed the major toward the site of the dogs' attempted excavations.

"Let's find out."

Picking up a scrap of splintered timber, Revell scraped aside a few clods of earth. Within a moment his efforts revealed a forearm, then the remainder of the limb. A little more effort uncovered the remainder of the body.

"Hell, those dogs have been making a meal of it." Above the bloodstained collar of a civilian jacket, the corpse's throat was almost severed. Ragged edges of flesh surrounded a wound that exposed shattered vertebrae.

"They hadn't dug down to it yet." Reveil knelt to make a closer examination, wrapping his scarf across his face against the stench. "This was done by a bullet, heavy caliber, fired from very close range."

"I can see something underneath it, Major. Can I have that length of wood."

Ripper worked hard for several minutes, finally levering the body aside. It flopped over onto its front, to reveal portions of at least two more beneath it.

"Jesus, what have we lit on here?" Ripper looked at the dimensions of the plot, and lifted his feet uneasily, as he realized the ground gave beneath them. It had an almost springy consistency, like standing on a really deep mattress. "You don't think they're all in here, do you. Better then two thousand civvies?"

"Could be." Revelled indicated the first body, the one the ravenous dogs had been after. "He must have been the last of the working party the Commies used to do the heavy work. If they'd made a better job of burying him we'd probably never have stumbled across this . . . this war crime."

"So what we going to do about it, Major? We ain't just going to let it alone, are we? Let them get away with it?"

"No way. This time we've got the Reds dead to rights. This territory has been in their hands for better than a year. Soon as we get back I'll slap in a report. Then we stand back, well back. Come the morning there are going to be a lot of very excited people running about here."

"The one thing we don't want is for anyone to get excited." Not even unfastening his seat belt, the senator spoke to Revell through the open cabin door of the Blackhawk helicopter. "How many of you men know about this . . . this incident."

The use of that carefully considered last word put Revell on his guard immediately. "All of them. Is there some reason it should have been kept quiet?"

Behind the politician, visible only as dark outlines in the shadow of the cabin, were two other figures.

"You're here to investigate, aren't you. Lay the blame for this where it belongs?" Having watched a squad of fatigue-clad civilians uncovering the charnel pit, Revell was at a loss to understand why they had stopped work at that point, and stood back. "What about identifying them, or autopsies . . . No one is even doing a body count."

Now some of the civilians were placing what looked like bulky incendiary devices at close spaced intervals across the top layer.

"What are they doing? How come there are no photographs being taken. Just what the hell is going on?"

One of the vague figures at the rear of the cabin leaned forward to whisper in the senator's ear. He returned an inaudible reply before turning again to Revell.

"No need to get excited, Major. Truth is we're not here as any sort of inquiry commission. In fact, officially we're not here at all."

"We're here . . ." Again the senator was involved in a muttered exchange with his unidentifiable companions . . . "We're here to impress upon you, and your men, that in the public interest news of your discovery must go no further. You and your outfit are doing a fine job, a fine job. But just you get on with what you're supposed to be doing and leave this little matter to us. It's all being taken care of."

"So why destroy the evidence without making any record of it?" A strong and ugly suspicion in Revell's mind was fast jelling into a certainty.

"What we have here, Major, is a serious health hazard . . ."

With an effort Revell kept his voice down, but he could not prevent an edge creeping into it. "Senator, we are not talking about violation of a city health code that you're fixing for a friend or relative. There are around two thousand dead people over there. The Reds did it, only a few days ago, so what are you intending to do about it?"

The senator's tone abruptly changed, from an ingratiating friendliness to hard impatience. "You've been told, Major. You go along with us in this or . . ."

"Perhaps I can deal with this, Senator."

Unbelting himself, one of the chopper's passengers alighted. Revell wasn't surprised, after hearing the accent, to see that it was a British officer. He was though, to see that he was a full-blown lieutenant general.

"Let's have a word in private, shall we, Major?" The general led away from the Blackhawk. "These damned civilians don't speak the same language as you and me."

"A mass grave, a war crime, carries the same meaning in any language, who ever says it, sir." Revell had made a quick scan of the general's medal ribbons. Of the twenty or so only two were combat or campaign decorations. The most recent was the Falklands ribbon, so for a long time the general had been a staff officer.

"Don't get clever, Major. I don't like it and won't put up with it. And you'd do well to heed the senator's words. He had a lot of people breathing down his neck on this. If he has to break you to keep this filthy mess under wraps, then that is what he will do."

"Why does it have to be kept under wraps anyway?"

"What we have here, Major, is a very delicate situation. I've had a word with your CO, Colonel Lippincott. Not a man to mince words. He said he spoke to you only recently. Says he gave you some idea of the big picture. I get the impression he considers you to be rather a wild man, but that he admires your fighting qualities."

"You were saying it was a delicate situation."

"So I was. And you had best believe it. Not that I'm involved in the PR side of things, but every general officer has to bear such implications in mind. There has been a lot of difficulty selling the idea of a truce to the population in Europe's unoccupied territories and in the U.S. When we were tagging along behind the Warpac retreat the press laid it on rather too thick. Gave every armchair strategist the impression that we had them beaten."

It was tempting, Revell almost interrupted with the names of his men who had been killed or disabled while "tagging along" behind the Warpac withdrawal.

"So consequently when we signed the truce papers there was a considerable body of opinion that couldn't grasp why, if we had them on the ropes, we didn't put them down for a count."

"A puzzle that was not confined to civilians, sir."

"Quite. The whole blasted thing is not made any easier by the Communists already having committed three flagrant breaches of the truce. And that is in the first forty-eight hours. What we don't need are the spectacular headlines your find would create. Stoke the fires of the public's righteous indignation only a little higher and we'll all get singed. Are you with me?"

"Every dirty inch of the way."

"Yes, I could see you were getting up the senator's

nose. Don't try to do the same to me. I understand you've upset one general already this week. You won't get away with it a second time."

"Do you expect my men to stand by and see this murder swept under the carpet?"

"That is exactly what I want them to do. What they'll be ordered to do by you."

Picking a sprig of heather, the general gazed to where final preparations were being made for the destruction of the remains of the refugee victims. "Look, Major. I find this business every bit as distasteful as you do. But you and I know that if the damned politicians smother this episode, the Communists will get caught out doing the same or worse elsewhere."

"Who's the third passenger?" Revell could see that the senator was once again in earnest conversation with the unseen member of the delegation.

"The one doing the nudging and whispering? Not too sure myself. A big noise in the West German coalition government I believe, high up in the Green Party. Acts and speaks more alike a deep pink to my way of thinking."

"Will this ever be made public?"

The general shrugged. "Who knows, perhaps when the truce collapses a few lines will be issued."

"Then it'll be swamped by other stories. Won't even make the back page."

"You're catching on, Major."

"What about your workforce. Can you be sure they'll keep their mouths shut?" Revell almost gagged as an eddy of wind brought the stench of the charnel pit. He noticed some of the men in fatigues were taking off their respirators and throwing up. "How have you explained it to them?"

"We don't have to explain the situation to them, any more than we needed to in your case. Far as they're concerned they're simply clearing up a mass grave after an epidemic. The reason we made a point of seeing you is that you and your bunch of cowboys have a reputation for writing your own orders. In this case I'm telling you it is not going to happen. You've got an order. You'll follow it to the letter."

At the bottom of the valley the first of the charges detonated. There was no noise, just a sudden eruption of dense white smoke. It had hardly begun to spread on the light breeze when another followed it, and then others at three second intervals.

The pall merged to hide the surface of the grave, then began to turn dark at its base as the furnace heat of the thermite ignited the corpses.

On the far side of the valley the last of the fatigue party were boarding a battle-weary Huey. As the last of them scrambled aboard, the chopper lifted, creating a local storm of twigs and dust. The ferocious downdraft gusted the bonfire smoke toward the officers.

"When we flew in," the general took out a handkerchief and made as if to hold it over his mouth and nose, then decided against it, "we passed over the Russian battalion you're supervising."

Revell sensed there was more to the general's remark than a mere polite observation. He expected there was more to come and waited, not expecting good news.

"You seem to have them working well. I know that's not easy. But if I were you, I'd get them to slow down. The chances are that with both sides needing this truce it could, despite everything, continue for quite a while."

"We've ten days to finish this work, then we go back."

"I'm afraid it's not quite that straightforward, Major Revell." The general dabbed at his streaming eyes with a corner of his handkerchief as the acrid smoke swept about them.

"As I said, your combat company has an unfortunate reputation in some circles. And of course the fewer people in circulation who know about this discovery, the more likely it is to stay a secret . . ."

"So we are going to be left to rot out here until the truce is over, and what we know can't be an embarrassment to anyone."

"Those are not the words I would have chosen to use, Major, but they convey the gist of the idea, except in one respect. The time scale. Two days, two weeks, two months: who knows how long the truce is going to last. What I can tell you, though, is that if it lasts two years you'll still be stuck out here. And there are no guarantees about you returning then."

"Seems like my combat company has got enemies on both sides."

"How right you are, Major. How very right you are."

Chapter 14

"What are we looking for?" Sergeant Hyde stood with the major and watched the progress of the excavation.

The explosion that had buried the bunker had loosened all the surrounding soil and the Russians were having to shore-up as they dug deeper.

"I want to find out what Warpac unit was here when that happened." He knew he didn't have to explain what "that" was.

"Then we should know soon." Hyde shouted a warning to the diggers and they scrambled clear as a side wall of the pit collapsed. "Fairly soon, that is." He had to shout again to get them back to work, and away from the water bucket. "Pity no one at HQ can tell us; this has taken fifty men off the work on the road."

"Maybe they could, but I've a feeling our radio traffic will be monitored for a while, to make sure we're being good boys and not telling tales out of school." Revell impatiently watched the men making a clumsy chore of re-fixing the shoring.

One of Vokes's pioneers jumped down to join them,

and by pushing one man, and threatening another with a huge fist, and a torrent of incomprehensible Dutch, got the task done in half the time.

"This way no one finds out we've been making inquiries, and maybe takes away our radio and transport."

"Major, major sir."

The call came from an excavation on the far side of the site.

Grigori, with an air of self-appointed authority, was supervising the removal of a body from beneath splintered logs that had formed a bunker's roof. They were smoked-stained on what had been the underside and soot coated much of the corpse.

A loop of razor wire girdling the woman's torso had to be cut before the remains could be hauled clear. The fractured end of a thigh bone projected from flesh that was fast decomposing.

"You won't mind, Major, if I point out that I'm trained to work on patients who aren't turning green at the edges and have maggots coming out of their nose." Distastefully, Sampson pushed the body over to examine the back, then let it roll face up again.

"No external signs I can see. Could have been anything, poison of some sort, heart attack . . ."

"What about the leg?" Revell could smell the woman, a heavy, cloying, sweet stench that he knew all too well.

Sampson hardly glanced at the ugly injury. "No bleeding, must have happened after death, when the roof came in on top of her." He pointed to discolored and crinkled patches of flesh. "Those are flash burns, from when they blew in the entrance, I should say." Pausing, he looked again at the exposed bone and then the pattern of the burns. "Of course I'm no Quincy, but

I'd say when it happened she was standing or more likely hanging up, like a wall ornament."

"Keep them digging." Placing a scrap of torn cloth over the face, Revell addressed the instruction to Old William, but it was Grigori who chimed in with a response.

"I will get them on it right away, Major, right . . ."

"You'll get your fat ass down there with the others." Revell rounded on the elderly Dutchman in charge of the excavation. "Keep them working, especially him."

Old William looked up from where he sat crosslegged on the ground. Slowly and very methodically he was filling a meershaum pipe. His Russian workers would frequently snatch a greedy and envious glance at him, as the best part of half an ounce was gradually thumbed into the capacious bowl.

"Ya." He nodded in agreement and went on with his private labors.

"It would speed things up if we took more men off the road." Hyde knew that was already in his officer's mind. "If the general was right about the truce, and we are going to be here for a while, it can't do any harm." He saw Revell was undecided. "I and the men want to know who did it, as well."

"Take another twenty. Concentrate most of them here, and have her buried and the grave marked."

"Not much to put on the cross." Hyde was grateful for once that he had no sense of smell.

"Just the cross will do. It'll be more than she had before."

Grigori sorted through the pieces of paper on the

map table. Some were no more than torn scraps, others were creased and dirty larger fragments, edges darkened and made brittle by flame that had licked them.

"This is not much with which to work, Major."

"Those fragments are all we've got so far, maybe all we'll get. Make as much sense out of them as you can."

The Russian bent to scrutinize the finds by the harsh glare of a single unshaded bulb.

Into the confined space of the lean-to tent, slung against the side of the Hummer, had crowded Revell and Vokes, along with Sergeant Hyde, as well as the Russian deserter.

"Ah, these are all a part of a single document." With purpose now, no longer moving the pieces at aimless random, Grigori began to assemble the parts of a torn message pad leaf.

"Yes, it is an order to withdraw. See, here is the time of transmission and receipt, the time withdrawal is to commence . . ." Peering over the top of wire-rimmed bifocals, Grigori scanned the other fragments. "Some of it is missing."

"Well tell us what we've got. Who is it addressed to, for a start." Revell was impatient with the man's fussing.

"Of course, Major. It is addressed to the commander of a unit . . ." Snatching off his glasses, folding them with a snap, Grigori tried to push his way out.

Revell grabbed him. "You're not diving out now. What does it say? What unit?"

Failing in a second attempt to escape from the canvas shelter, Grigori allowed himself to be pushed back to the table. It was as if he had shrunk within himself. The overlay of brash self-confidence had been torn away.

"You don't want to know, Major. Let us just get on

with the task we have. I will work especially hard . . ."

That the man was scared was all too obvious. He wasn't acting. It was hard for Revell to imagine what could have such an effect on such a tough character.

"Tell us who the message was for."

"It was . . . It was for a Colonel Tarkovski." Grigori crossed himself as he uttered the name.

"This is no time to be reverting to religion." In a dim recess of his mind Revell vaguely recalled the name, but couldn't quite place it. "So what unit is it?"

Grigori lowered his voice to a hoarse whisper, so that the three of them had to bend close to catch his words.

"It is addressed to Colonel Tarkovski, commanding officer of Disciplinary Battalion 717. They have a private name for themselves, Beria's Sons."

"Means nothing to me." Vokes had noted the awe, amounting almost to fear in their Russian's voice, and the looks Hyde and Revell had exchanged. "What can be so special about them? Surely a punishment battalion would be employed by the Soviets simply as cannon fodder."

"Not this one." Revell handed Grigori a dusty roll of adhesive tape. "Piece it together as best you can with that."

"Who is Beria?" Vokes persisted.

Taking a bottle from a locker, Revell poured three glasses, and then as an afterthought a glass for the Russian. "He was Stalin's head of secret police. Almost grabbed power when his boss died. It's suspected he helped Stalin on his way. Didn't do himself any good though. He was shot in one of the cells of the Lubyanka eventually."

"That still does not explain what is special about this

battalion."

Hyde downed the gin in one go, not tasting it until it touched the back of his throat, and then only as a mildly burning sensation. "For a start, Lieutenant, it's the KGB's own punishment unit. Run by them, for then. All of them, even officers, are men who have just avoided being shot or hung, or were reprieved to make up numbers when the battalion fell below strength. Between them they committed every crime and every atrocity you can imagine, and if you're lucky, a lot that you can't."

"I had imagined the KGB was above the law." Vokes held out his glass for an offered refill.

"They are." Grigori had finished his drink and now rolled the glass between his palms. "But they have a system of internal discipline to take care of those who do not fit. They are men who even among the company of executioners and perverts stand out. I think in many cases they are hardly human."

"Do you think our high-powered visitors knew of this?"

"Whether they did or not, Lieutenant," Revell hesitated, then sent Grigori out, with a warning to keep quiet. "Whether they did or not, I don't think it would have made a blind bit of difference. All that matters to them is the truce. That's why they brought no press, no PR men with them. As far as they're concerned the incident is closed. Two thousand civvies, so what, sometimes ten times that number have died in a day, caught up in a battle."

"Nothing we can do about it?" Picking up a sheet of graph paper with the fragments stuck to it, Hyde re-read the transcription their translator had scrawled in the margin. Turning to a plastic overlaid wall map, he traced the KGB unit's known withdrawal route.

"We lack the resources, even if we knew where they were." Revell switched on a second lamp for a better view of the map. "OK, so we know the way they went, but not where they stopped. They could be just the other side of the demilitarized strip or back in Moscow by now."

"Would it be so difficult to find out?"

Revell considered Vokes's question. "At this time, yes. With no fighting going on and no fresh prisoners coming in, tactical intelligence gathering will have come almost to a stop. As far as I'm aware, even reconnaissance flights are forbidden, manned or unmanned. I presume the satellites will still be gathering more information than anyone can use, but among the mass of Warpac troops a comparatively small unit like the 717th will be undetectable."

"What about electronic intelligence gathering?" Hyde persisted. "They can often pinpoint who is where. HQ should have access to the data; haven't we got any contacts?"

With the tip of his forefinger Revell obliterated the fiber-pen marked track that Hyde had added to the map. "I know what you're thinking, but we'll have to forget it. For the duration we're road menders, nothing more. Tarkovski and 717th are probably a long way from here. They're nothing to do with us now."

Chapter 15

The old farmhouse resounded with the sounds and echoes of hammering. Tarkovski ignored the noise. He had swept plates and cutlery and the dust of a long abandoned meal from the top of a plain pine kitchen table. Now it was spread with a huge map of the area. On top of that lay a clutch of aerial photographs.

Several of his officers watched as the colonel impatiently sifted through them. They neither moved or made any comment. Even a mighty crash from the room above, as a heavy beam of timber was dropped, elicited no response from them. They did not even make any effort to brush away the cloud of dust-laden cobwebs that settled on them.

The light in the room was gradually diminishing as a sandbag wall rose higher outside the window. Tarkovski ignored that also, continuing to shuffle through the large glossy prints. Finally he selected one for examination through a large magnifying glass.

"Whose responsibility was it to see the disposal of the bodies?"

"Ensign Fastenko, Comrade Colonel."

Tarkovski didn't look up. He knew who had spoken, recognized the distinctive lisp. He should know, it was he who had knocked out his second-in-command's front teeth at their first meeting. The major had been under the impression he'd drawn an easy assignment. A pick-handle across his face had swiftly disabused him of that notion.

"You mean Private Fastenko I think." Tarkovski let the words sink in. "Private Fastenko who is now on permanent latrine duty."

"Yes, Comrade Colonel."

"You were going to add something?" Still Tarkovski didn't look up.

"What of Captain . . . what of Private Chulpenyev. That has been his post."

"Give him something more interesting to do. Find him some mines to clear." For the first time Tarkovski lifted his gaze from the photograph. "Unless any of you have an urge to join him, I suggest you turn your minds to this." He held the photograph out toward them and slowly panned it before the faces of the group.

"Look carefully. It shows that a shitty little NATO battalion has been rooting around in what was until recently our property. We would not have known except that by luck I was passed these." He smacked the pile of prints, sending several onto the floor.

The sandbag barricade had risen higher. Occasionally the grimy faces and arms of the the civilians building it could be seen.

Tarkovski ignored them, as he continued to ignore the construction work overhead. "I take it very personally when damned Yanks or British shits start rummaging through my garbage pits. I would like them deterred from doing it any more."

All of the officers knew that by this time of day the colonel would be well into his second bottle of vodka. On a sideboard stood not only that half empty bottle, but also an open Georgian brandy. It was when Tarkovski mixed his drinks that he was at his most dangerous. His rigid stance, slow and deliberate speech and unfocused stare confirmed how far gone he was. They waited for a definite cue, before daring to offer any suggestions.

"I want it done tonight. And I don't want anything traceable back to us to be left behind."

"The second platoon of the first company is at full strength, Colonel. They have done such raids before. Their commander would be perfect for such a task."

With difficulty the major suppressed a smile of deep satisfaction. It would be an ideal opportunity for him to dispose of the senior lieutenant in question. The man was becoming greedy, insisting on an equal share of the huge profits to be made from their hoard of Afghan hashish.

Of course he could not be certain that the lieutenant would be killed in the night action. He had already noted in him a considerable talent for self-preservation. No, one could not leave such things to chance. As insurance, to make absolutely sure, he would brief Junior Sergeant Ivanov to take care of him in the inevitable confusion of withdrawal.

The sergeant was ambitious, and hoping for promotion. And he would enjoy such work. He was in the battalion in the first place for beating a Polish officer almost to death. Not that, for a Russian, that was much of a crime, but the man had been a general, and a political officer at that . . . that had just tipped the balance against him, where otherwise a KGB man could have felt himself safe from military justice.

"They will require transport, Colonel."

"The hell they will. Have they got no feet?"

"It was just that the Comrade Colonel said he wanted the action to pass without detection of its source. Surely if the men can be extricated quickly and cleanly afterward . . . ?" The major left the sentence hanging.

"And where do you think the fuel is coming from? Three of the trucks are dry, and I've only half a tank in the field car."

That was a lie, about the field car at least. The major knew the trucks were out of gas as they'd been siphoned to replenish the colonel's personal transport.

"I believe I can find sufficient fuel, Colonel."

Tarkovski knew his second-in-command meant he knew where he could steal some, from another unit. Or perhaps he'd trade some of his stockpile of hash if he had to, if there was no other way to obtain it.

"Very well, take the damned trucks. Just make sure you bring them all back. And one last thing." Tarkovski leaned against the table to steady himself, his eyes constantly wandering to the brandy. "I want the maximum number of casualties inflicted on those shitty road diggers. I want the crap scared out of them, so they don't go sticking their dirty NATO noses into what isn't their business, anymore. Now beat it, the lot of you."

As the last of his officers left, Tarkovski stumbled to the sideboard and sloshed a large measure of brandy into a plastic cup. Some of the spirit oozed through a fine split in its side as he grabbed it up and tossed it back.

"Where the hell is my orderly." He bellowed at the wall.

Into the gloom of the darkening room came a stoop-shouldered private, clutching a grease-stained message pad.

"Here, Comrade Colonel."

Staring at the faded floral print of the wallpaper inches from his nose, Tarkovski belched. His mind was not so clouded by drink that he could not recall an important point from the recent exchange.

"Make out a charge against the major."

The clerk waited for several minutes, then timidly prompted.

"What section shall I put it under, Comrade Colonel?"

Tarkovski considered the question. He thought of the major's hoard of hashish. It was as well to be thorough. "Make it section forty two, subsection three. Failure to disclose holdings of vital war supplies. Namely fuel."

"Does the Comrade Colonel wish to give the verdict now?" He knew he hardly need ask, but the clerk poised his pen, not writing the inevitable until the C.O. spoke.

"Guilty of course, you shithead."

"And the sentence, Comrade Colonel?"

For a moment Tarkovski considered. Not the sentence. That would be death as a matter of course. "By hanging I think. We might as well save the few rounds a firing squad would use, and besides," he poured himself another glass, "I like to see them mess their pants as I kick the chair away."

"Is there anything else, Comrade Colonel?"

The orderly was backing away, as if in fear that on a

sudden whim of the officer he might find himself keeping the major company, creating double the foul entertainment.

"No. Wait, yes there is, now I come to think of it."

Only a small gap was left for daylight to enter the room, between the damp smelling sandbags. It made a searchlight-like beam across the dusty interior.

"How many refugee camps are there in this area? What's the intelligence estimate of the number of displaced persons?"

"Three settlements within six miles, Comrade Colonel. I think the figure is three hundred."

"Think? You *think?* I want to bloody well know!" Tarkovski waved the cringing orderly's excuses aside. "Never mind, stop wetting yourself."

Leaning back against the wall, Tarkovski felt the room beginning to rotate about him. It was a feeling he loved and he savored the first moments of disorientation.

"The few lazy shits we've rounded up so far are worse than useless. I want this place bomb-proof this week, not next year. Have more rounded up. A couple of hundred adults should do it."

The orderly made to leave, hesitating in the doorway when he thought he caught a fragment of mumbled instruction. "Did the colonel want something more?"

"Are you deaf? I said date that arrest for tomorrow. I'll let the major enjoy tonight. If all goes well, he'll think he's sitting pretty for a while. I'd like the turnaround in his fortunes to be all the more upsetting."

"Is that all, Comrade Colonel?"

"Yes, wait, no." Tarkovski braced his legs, to stop himself from sliding down. "It's Tuesday today. Have all those filthy refugees collected. Every last one. I'm in the mood for a bit of fun. Have them all here on Saturday. We'll have another of our parties."

Chapter 16

Night exploded into sharp stark white light as a star-shell burst high above the clearing. By contrast the surrounding woods were all the darker. Curving lines of green and orange tracer flashed out from among the depths of the trees.

Shouts and screams came from a tent as bullets punched close spaced holes in the canvas at waist height. Another was already alight, and men reeled from it, flapping at blazing clothing.

A mortar shell detonated behind the Hummer, slashing its adjoining lean-to into ribbons and starting a fire among spare fuel cans lashed to the back.

Shocked awake by the concussion, Revell rolled clear as the flames engulfed the tinder dry material. He was scrambling to his feet five meters away when the transport's fuel tank erupted in a ball of flame and he was put down again.

The body he landed beside still clutched an M16. Revell grabbed it, and loosed off the whole magazine toward the source of the tracer.

There was no noticeable effect. A second magazine achieved no better result. He looked around. The clearing was lit like day. Although the flare had sunk from sight, the fires more than compensated for its disappearance.

Others were returning the fire, but there was no diminution in the bursts of lethal incoming. On the far side of the Russian compound a truck took a direct hit and scything slivers of cab and engine casing brought down more tents. They collapsed, like shrouds, over the dead and dying within.

Several bodies hung on the surrounding wire. The only men moving were the wounded, who did so involuntarily, and those who crawled and hugged the ground in search of cover.

"They're using dark ignition tracer. Shift your fire further in among the timer." Revell had to shout to be heard, but his information was passed on.

Andrea crashed to the ground beside him, seeking the slight shelter offered by the corpse. She leveled her rifle and used its underslung grenade launcher to launch a succession of 40mm rounds into the woods.

Watching the flat trajectory of the incoming tracer, Revell made a mental projection back to its probable point of origin. With its tell-tale flare not visible until it was fifty meters or more from the weapon firing it, he could only at best make an educated guess.

The first half-dozen rounds he fired from the third magazine bounced harmlessly from an unseen tree. Then he got lucky. There was no sign to give away a point of impact, but suddenly a line of tracer flicked skyward.

Updrafts generated by the several fierce fires were

sending a rain of fiery scraps into the trees, starting secondary conflagrations that threatened to merge and spread.

A last mortar bomb exploded among a tangle of bodies close by the wire, and then Revell realized the attack had ceased. It was over. As abruptly as it had started. Gradually at first, and then rapidly, the returning fire petered out and finally ceased.

An eerie, momentary silence ensued. Then against a background of crackling small arms ammunition cooking off, came the all too audible cries and moans of the wounded.

"These poor sods caught the worst of it." Sergeant Hyde walked with the two officers through what was left of the Russian compound.

Only two tents still stood. The growing illumination of dawn revealed the other previous sites marked by blackened circles of ground. Thirty bodies lay in a close spaced row. Most were roughly draped with greatcoats. A couple had only their faces covered. One with a piece of cardboard from a ration box, the other a gouged and dented door panel from a truck.

The fires aboard the vehicles had burned out, but in among the trees men could be heard beating at the still smoldering underbrush.

Vokes examined a large tattered piece of what looked like red and black chiffon caught on the wire. He was glad he had not instinctively reached to touch it, when he realized what it in fact was.

He twanged the wire, and the patch of burnt skin that had sloughed from some victim of the blazing encampment fluttered to the ground.

"It could have been much worse." Vokes wrinkled his nose as they repassed the line. Fluids from the dead were soaking into the ground about several of them. Large numbers of flies were already being attracted. "I have lost only two men killed. And that because, against my orders, they were sleeping aboard their vehicle." He looked to where attempts were being made to lever free the remains from metalwork fire had welded them to.

"We lost six." Revell paused by the wire, close by the bodies of his men. "Would have been less, but they tried to keep the Ruskies from getting out. They must have stood out like range targets, standing with those fires behind them."

"Have the sentries been found yet?" Vokes slapped at a large blue-bottle that persisted mindlessly in repeatedly buzzing his face.

"No. One of the patrols will find them." Constantly Revell was interrogating himself. What had he failed to do, and how many lives had each omission cost?

His own men, and Vokes's, had dug slit trenches almost as a matter of habit. But nothing they'd tried could induce the construction battalion to do the same. They had paid dearly for their lethargy. Beside the thirty dead were another fifty injured. A high proportion had serious burns. Many of them would not survive. He saw that Lippincott was beckoning him over to his high-sided Saxon command vehicle.

"There was nothing more you could have done, Major," was the only support Vokes could offer as he left them. Under his breath, to himself, he added, "but in their eyes it will not have been enough."

"Hell, you really do seem to find trouble just about everywhere you go, don't you, Major." Lippincott drummed his teeth with the well-chewed end of a pencil.

"I'd say this time it found us."

Lippincott ignored the rejoinder. "You have no idea how much trouble these casualties of yours are causing us. It was a good thing I was already on my way here when I got the call. If I hadn't been on hand to smooth matters, then no powers on earth could have saved your commission. Just at the time the best thing you and your maniacs can do is to lie low, you've got to try and create another damned incident."

"I won't accept that, Colonel. We can't take the blame for a sneak attack by some Warpac outfit."

"There you go again." Pausing to chew hard for a moment. "Whatever you do, Major, when the war is over, if you survive it, don't go into the diplomatic corps."

"Do you have some other explanation, then?"

"A thousand that will go down better with the generals and politicians than that. Any case, what makes you think that in all the Zone, packed as it is with tanks and dumps and troops, the Reds are going to risk a truce they want by hitting your tin-pot outfit?"

"Likely or not, that's what it must have been . . ."

"A regular Warpac unit? Never. No, what I reckon we've got here is a hit by an armed refugee mob. After your food, or ammunition. Or maybe it was one of those renegade bands, you know the type. Made up of assorted deserters of every nationality. They'll take on anything if there's a profit in it."

"For anyone who wasn't here, that's a plausible explanation. For anyone who wants the truce kept going it's also a damned convenient one." Revell felt he was crashing his head against a brick wall. He tried to keep the frustration and resentment out of his tone.

"It was bad enough to find cast iron evidence of a war crime and be told to do nothing about it, even be threatened with drastic consequences if I so much as dared to breathe a word about it. And now this. Six of my men dead, two of Lieutenant Vokes's pioneers as well. We've ten wounded, including one who won't see again and another with his bottom jaw shot off. And there's those poor bloody Ruskies. They weren't even armed."

"You've made your point, but your orders stand. You stay here, you keep your heads down. That way, given time, maybe I can sort of rehabilitate you in the eyes of the general, but for God's sake give me a bit of cooperation."

On the road the ambulance convoy was getting ready to move out. Doors were being secured. Its heavy escort of military police outriders were jockeying into position.

"Where are you taking them?" Revell felt he had to change the subject or he'd explode with frustration. Ten years of taking orders had never prepared him for this.

"I said your casualties were causing problems. Take a look at that convoy and believe it. Strings were pulled that I didn't know existed to assemble that inside of four hours. Couldn't evacuate them by chopper in case one went down somewhere and tales got told. Had to be an overland job, where we could keep an eye on everyone.

I've lined them up a whole wing of a high-security isolation hospital, other side of Hanover. Never thought I'd be back bossing a convoy at this rank." Lippincott started on another pencil.

"Sure as hell I didn't think my butt would be on the line if I screwed up."

While they'd talked, the dead had been body-bagged and now the last of them was slid into the back of a large closed truck.

"I've still two men unaccounted for; we had sentries down the road a half kilometer." As they walked to convoy, Revell kept an eye on the direction by which his patrols would return.

"Not much chance you'll find them alive." Lippincott climbed up into the Saxon's open rear doorway. "When they turn up, bury them here. Make a note for graves registration . . ."

"I'll radio it in."

"The fuck you will. As of now you're under strict radio silence. If the Warpac 3rd Shock Army come steaming this way, you run and tell us."

"If this keeps up, the only one of us to leave here will have patted down the soil on all the others." Sampson turned away from the two graves.

Grigori had appointed himself overseer of the grave-diggers. He now fussily supervised the filling in of the two excavations.

Revell made no reply to their medic. He felt worn out, pulled down by the utter futility of their situation. The bodies had been found shortly after the ambulances had departed. They had been buried with the minimum of ceremony in a small clearing away from the site of the enemy position, where the trees and ground were undamaged by fire and explosion.

Though it was still an hour to midday the sun was already making them uncomfortable. The dust that had percolated through their clothing mixed with their sweat into a kind of grinding paste that itched mercilessly.

Revell looked forward to a chance to strip and wash later in the day. If the patrols had found no sign of their attackers, other than a lot of empty cartridge cases, at least one of them had found a small lake. Largely free of contamination, it was only a couple of kilometers away. Dooley had been sent out with a couple of the pioneers to find and mark a direct route to it.

If they were to be stuck here for a considerable length of time, Revell saw no reason why they shouldn't at least be as comfortable as possible. It would be some, if a very small, consolation.

Dooley appeared, running at his best speed. He had to gasp and gulp air before he could articulate.

"We've found a wounded civvy. Could be one of the hit men from last night. He's in a bad way."

"How far?"

"About ten minutes, on foot. No hope of getting a truck there."

"Right, lead the way." Revell called to their medic. "Sampson, bring two stretcher bearers. At the double." A thought occurred to him. Carrington was close by. "Corporal, grab Grigori, follow as fast as you can."

The route was through virgin forest, a compass course that detoured only around the most impenetrable tangles of undergrowth.

Despite having already run the journey once, Dooley set a fast pace, stumbling through and crushing down any shrubbery that had sprung upright since his last passage.

When they reached him, the wounded man had been hauled to a half-sitting position against the trunk of a tree. Apart from that, the two Dutchmen standing guard had done nothing to help him.

"Where did we get him?" The reclining man's clothes were so saturated in blood that Revell could not determine where he had been wounded. He waited for the corpsman to complete a hurried examination.

"Not us, Major." Turning the man half to his side, Sampson pulled a long, slim bladed knife from just beneath his right shoulder blade. "Nice crowd he was mixing with."

Conscious, but white-faced with pain and shock, the man looked up at the officer. His mouth opened and closed soundlessly as he tried to form words. He succeeded only in producing pink bubbles that trickled down the sides of his chin to drip slowly onto his chest.

"Someone really wanted him dead." Sampson stood up. "I count three stabs wounds in the back, another through the throat. He's dying fast, Major, only a few minutes at most. You want me to give him a shot, help him go easy?"

Beckoning Grigori forward, Revell knelt down beside the dying man. "Tell him he is dying . . ."

"Hasn't he had enough . . ."

Revell shut off Sampson's protest and signaled to Grigori to go ahead. Limply, without change of expression the man acknowledged what he was told. "Tell him we want to get the men who hit our camp last night, and that it means we'll get the backstabber who did this to him."

That took longer, and Revell listened to the largely incomprehensible flow. The dying man appeared to have trouble grasping what was said to him, and the major had their interpreter repeat his words twice more.

After a moment, the effort bringing bubbles of pink blood to his lips, the man began to splutter a reply, each word accompanied by audible bubblings from his chest. It took time, with frequent pauses to gather what little strength and breath he had left. Finally his words were reduced to an incoherent mumble. He sagged lower against the tree, gasping like a fish out of water. What air he did manage to suck into his pain-wracked frame could be heard whistling out through the holes in his lungs.

Grigori appeared indifferent to the man's suffering, looking on him with contempt. "He is a senior lieutenant in the KGB, I did not catch his name, but it is unimportant. His unit is the 717. They are at a farm ten kilometers down the road, right on the edge of the demilitarized Zone."

"Is that all?" Revell had been only able to understand the odd word or two, and was unsure how much he could trust their interpreter, or if he should at all. "There seemed to be more than that."

"The ramblings of a dying man." Grigori shrugged. "There was talk of hashish, and another officer, and of a junior sergeant. That name I did catch, he repeated it many times, Ivanov."

"Anything else?"

"Only that it is his wish we kill them all."

"Not much loyalty among Communists, is there."

"Oh, no, Major," Grigori took the remark at face value, missing the irony. "Absolutely none."

Chapter 17

"Fucking creeps." Dooley kicked out at a Russian who had stopped work to scratch his backside, and missed.

"I thought they were working quite well today." Scully accepted the end of the hawser and passed it to a pioneer who stood on top of the felled tree.

"No, not this lot. I mean those animals back at HQ. The major has told them who did that dirty work over at the camp, and where they are now. And what do they do, fuck all."

Taking the end of the wire as it was pushed back beneath the timber, Dooley made it fast to form a loop about the thick trunk.

"I suppose they know what they're doing."

Scully began shepherding the Russians clear before the slack was taken up. The cable had already parted once and they'd been lucky not to have any serious injuries from the incident.

"Do they? Letting the Reds get away with the murder of a couple of thousand civvies don't seem right to me, no way. They did in Afghanistan, no reason why they should get away with it here."

From a safe distance they watched the truck edging forward. Gradually the coil of steel straightened out. In his cab, Burke kept a close watch on the door mounted rear view mirror. Guided by hand signals from Lieutenant Vokes, he applied the brakes as soon as the full length of the plaited wire was suspended above the ground. It vibrated, with a low pitched twanging sound, in time with the slow throb of the idling motor.

Vokes went forward to the cab door, shouting in through the open window.

"Take it very slowly. Stay on the line I showed you, across the road, then between those two trees and over the little clearing beyond. The going is soft, but I think it is just the deep layer of leafmold. Try not to stop, or you may dig-in."

This was the first of the trees to be tackled by the towing method and a crowd was gathering to watch. For the NATO soldiers it was pure curiosity; the Russian laborers though had a more specific interest. If it worked there would be less heavy work for them to tackle.

There was almost an air of excitement as the truck edged forward, accompanied by the creaking of the hawser, the splintering of wood and the deep bellow of the straining engine.

For a long moment there was no apparent movement, and a half-derisive cheer went up from the assembled audience. It was repeated when the truck began to crab sideways on the dusty surface.

A sharp crack was accompanied by a fountain of bark as the wire slipped a meter along the trunk, cutting cleanly through the stumps of several small branches. The truck's exhaust boomed louder and almost imperceptibly the obstacle began to move. It pivoted slowly around the soil-encrusted mountain of its roots, moving steadily.

Attention switched abruptly back to the truck as its motor suddenly cut out. Sunk to its axles on one side, half way across the clearing, it rested at an angle of forty-five degrees.

Burke jumped down from the elevated cab step. "That's the first bloody crash I've ever had at two miles an hour."

Vokes circled the stranded vehicle. "No harm done. We'll pull it out. It just means that for the next go we shall have to lay some sort of roadway, then . . ."

He stopped talking and bent down to examine where a large chunky treaded tire had scooped away the topsoil.

"Give me something to dig with, quickly." He accepted the bayonet that was offered and began to carefully scrape more of the loosened material away.

Pushing his way through to the front rank, Revell looked down. The arm and shoulder, and then the head of a young child were exposed.

Reaching out, Revell pulled the lieutenant back. His work had already revealed another arm, to a body crushed beneath the wheel.

"Children." There was a deep, choking sadness in Vokes's voice. "In heavens name, how many will there be."

"There are two too many already." Leaving the encircling crowd, Clarence knelt beside the find and brushed soil from a small dirt-ingrained hand. "It just goes on and on, doesn't it."

For a while Revell had thought the men quite capable of bodily lifting the three-ton Bedford off the grave. It had taken considerable effort by himself and Hyde to push the others back.

"I want a guard on this site. No one is to touch anything."

"Right, Major. I'll put Clarence on first." Hyde knew there was no way he would be able to get the sniper to leave the scene in any event. "If he's going to be hanging about, he might as well be doing something useful."

"This an experience that will be good for him." Andrea ran his fingers along the ribbon that had been tied between the trees to mark off the ground.

"You really are a callous bitch." Hyde had no time for the girl, when she was drunk, or as now, surprisingly sober. She had a face men would kill for, but the mind behind it was filled with death, and needed no more. "It reminds him of his kids. He found them buried under what was left of his married quarters in Cologne."

"I know that." Untwisting a kink in the tape, Andrea flicked a moth from it. "Do you know that he has set himself a target? He is killing a hundred Russians for each of them, and for his wife. At that last count he told me he had only a few to go. Perhaps now he will start again. It will give him something to go on living for."

It was not what the major had expected her to come out with. His instinctive reaction to the discovery of the little bodies was to rush to headquarters and throw his news at them. A moment's calmer consideration told Revell it could achieve nothing. Next he wanted to get on the radio and tell the world, well as much as he could reach, what was happening. It was more than likely though that any calls he made would be monitored, and rapidly jammed.

Either course of action would fail to get worthwhile results, except maybe to bring down a storm of trouble on the whole unit.

He spent an hour thinking the situation through, then made his decision. It took another hour to write out the messages, then just a few minutes to get together couriers and escorts.

Armed with passes that would get them to their various destinations, the six teams departed, taking with them the best of the transport and all the fuel they had.

He was taking a huge gamble, but at least this way, at this stage, any repercussions would come back on him alone. It was too late even now to have second thoughts. There was no way he could pursue and turn back the dispatchers even if he'd wanted to. For all his determination though, he felt inside an unpleasant hollow, sick feeling.

Casting his thoughts back to what lay within the little, ribbon-enclosed clearing banished his doubts, and replaced it with anger and impatience.

"You getting married, and want me to make up an album? Is that it?" Swanson unslung his camera bag from his shoulder. "The boys you sent for me weren't exactly the chatty sort. Come to that, I thought they were a tight-lipped pair of miserable bastards."

Revell had to smile at the thought of Ripper being described as tight-lipped. "That was their orders. You'll pick up the background as you go along. The basics are that I want a complete photographic record of something that's happened here."

"No problem. Why all the mystery. Is it being sat on? Are you?"

"Yes to both, heavily. Will your boss miss you if you're missing for a half a day."

"So who runs photographic? I'm my own boss most of the time. We don't fit into any cozy little niche so we get left to do our own thing. Where do I start."

"There's a pit on the other side of the hill. It's been burned out, but thoroughly. There might just be a chance though that something is left. Perhaps a side caved in and covered a few pieces. Anyway, you'll have some laborers with you, they'll do the dirty work."

"Great, sounds fun. What then?"

"Back here. And this won't be."

"Oh my. I never want to see anything like this again." Swanson stalked about the edge of the deepening excavation, the motor on his camera making an almost continual whirring sound.

The truck had been gently pulled clear. Under close supervision the Russians were starting to remove the bodies. Twenty were laid in a neatly spaced row. More were being added all the time.

As each was carefully pulled from the deathly hold of others, even more were revealed. The excavation had grown almost to the full width of the small clearing.

"How soon can I have prints? And I'll want copies."

"I anticipated that a call from you wouldn't be for any ordinary event. In fact I rushed out here as a sort of advance guard. Here come the rest of my guys right now."

The distinctive double beat of a Chinook was becoming audible. Swanson delved into his pocket and extracted a signal candle.

"Could you have one of your men ignite that close by, that chewed up chunk of land beside the road will do. If there's a level space to set that down."

The giant twin rotor helicopter was hovering almost over them. Slung beneath it dangled a wheeled cabin with shuttered windows.

"It's a mobile developing room. Knew you'd be in a hurry as always, and this way I can guarantee privacy. Won't have to send or transmit any material. Oh yes, and they're bringing video cameras, complete with sound equipment. By the time I'm through you'll have the comprehensive record you wanted. And if you're going over to Division to ram it down the throat of whoever is keeping this under wraps, I'll film that for you as well."

Chapter 18

"Can you erect a screen of some description? This won't be pretty. No point in spoiling everybody's dinner." On a table made from stacked gas cans and broken planks, the surgeon was setting out a row of knives and saws.

"I'll have something rigged up right away." Revell looked at the shining instruments. "How many will you want . . . want to . . ." He couldn't think of the right words to use.

"How many have you exhumed so far?"

"About fifty so far, Doc, but it's going to go a lot higher."

"Five will give us a good sample. I hope you know what you're getting us all into."

"This has been forced on me, but I gave you the chance to cry off."

"Yes, yes, I know you did. Sorry, that wasn't fair. Right, I'll need an assistant with a strong stomach."

"There's Sampson, our medic. He should be a help."

"Hell, I don't need any help to do an autopsy. I want these blasted wasps swatted away from me. Can't stand the bloody pests. Prefer to work where there's an unhealthy dose of contamination in the air, keeps the garish little buggers down. Actually I will use your medic. It'll be good experience for him. At least he can watch."

"Anything else, Doc?" Revell ducked as a wild swing to fend off a fly nearly connected with the side of his head.

"Sorry, thought it was a wasp. Just can't stand the stupid things. Hate the way they creep up behind you and go 'buzz' in your ear when you're least expecting it. I don't suppose you've got anyone who can take dictation have you, possibly shorthand . . . no, silly question really."

"We have." Revell beckoned forward a bespectacled clerk. "This is Private Watts. Borrowed him from another Division's HQ. Been trying to get into this outfit for ages. Very keen, even brought his portable with him. He'll have your report typed out for checking before you go."

"Major, this wasn't quite what I had in mind," Watts adopted a pained expression. "Office work is what I do all the time. You said hazardous duty. I can't tell my girlfriend this is what I've been doing."

"You can't tell anyone what you've been doing, boy. If you do, you'll find out just how hazardous this is."

The surgeon pulled on long rubber gloves as a stretcher holding a light load, a child's remains, was brought to the table.

Revell noticed the sudden change of color in the young clerk's face. "You don't have to look."

"No, you bloody don't. Take forever to do these autopsies if you keep fainting all over the place. Fall on the table and I might do you before you know it."

The doc winked at Revell before squaring his shoulders, taking up a large knife and leaning over to make the first cut.

Watts didn't have time to look away. His head started to spin, before he realized that it was only the body's clothing being cut away.

"I thought you weren't going to look."

"I'm not going to." Watts caught a last glimpse of the skinny doll-like form on the table. He shuddered, and moved aside as an improvised canvas screen was erected about the table. "How do you ever get used to doing things like that?"

"You don't. Those that try to, go nuts. Me, I divorce myself from reality. For instance I wear frilly underwear and subscribe to *Readers Digest* before they send me junk mail."

"Are you serious, Doc?" After choosing a pen from a multi-colored selection lining his top pocket, Watts turned his notebook to a clean page.

"No, of course I'm not. I prefer part-works."

There was the rumble of heavy traffic from the road. A convoy of six-wheeled M-820s shouldered past the burnt-out Hummer and growled to a halt short of the felled trees. Their overhanging van bodies were festooned with masses of artificial camouflage, liberally supplemented by quantities of dead foliage, including whole saplings.

"Where do you want us, Major?"

"Hell." Revell scanned the line of trucks. "I wasn't expecting you to bring the whole outfit."

Captain Lee leaned from a cab window. The grin on his face disappeared when from his high vantage point he saw the work going on inside the screened off enclosure, and the seemingly endless lines of small bodies close by. "My CO is off on leave. I thought I'd take them all out on a tactical exercise. Pure coincidence I chose this area, of course."

"Here's the location we want scanned." Revell handed up a map. "I've marked it. Can do?"

"No problem." Lee tossed the folded paper to the corporal beside him in the cab. "Need to get a mite nearer though, and spread out a little. Looks like we'll have to do a spot of cross country motoring. These big brutes aren't so hot at that. Good thing we brought a wrecker. Now that is something that might be missed. It's the only good one in the Division. So how much information do you want?"

"What can you get for me?" Revell was distracted by the next truck in line. From the rear of its capacious body a tall telescopic mast was growing. At fifty feet, topping the highest trees, it stopped and the small dish atop it began to rotate.

"Ignore that. It'll be one of my sergeants getting the football results. He likes to show off with that thing. Has a sticker on the back of the truck that gets us into no end of hassle. Says 'Electronic Intelligence have longer ones than anyone else'."

"So what else can he get."

"Between us, anything. Give me twelve hours and I'll give you a printout on every power source, every emission and every transmission, to and from that area. You can have a breakdown of quantity and type of transport operating there and passing through. Usually we can pinpoint flak sites, radars, parking lots . . . you name it, we label it."

"Can you get me transcriptions of radio messages?"

"No problem. You'll be wanting the same of landline traffic as well, I suppose. We've got a couple of real hot interpreters who can take care of that."

"Good, get me the lot."

"Oh, one last thing. Last truck in the line isn't ours. I took the liberty of inviting him along. Royal Artillery, worked with him before. He's got one of those new mini-drones aboard, specializes in low level work, real low level. Uses real-time data transmission, so you'll get something even if by a miracle the Reds notice it and down it."

"We can use him. Thanks." Revell had to move to the side to make more room for the growing line of small corpses.

As each of the trucks made a three point turn, the crews looked out silently at the latest begrimed additions to the sad spectacle. He saw the grim expressions on the soldiers' faces, and knew he'd get every scrap of information he needed.

"You want me to sign them? Or shall I just go out and shoot myself now, save them the expense of doing it after they've finished throwing the book at me."

"No need for that. Will you keep one set of the copies? Put them away in a safe place." Revell leafed through the autopsy reports. "And thanks for your help."

"Save it. You can thank me if or when it helps you nail those Communist bastards."

The doc stripped off his thickly coated gloves and tossed them onto the pile of discarded clothing.

"In twenty-five years I've never seen anything like it. What those kids must have gone through. The one with the bullet through the side of his head was the lucky one. The others . . . well it's all in the reports. If there's anything else I can do?"

"Can't think of anything, Doc. You'd better scoot now. You haven't even got a lame excuse for being here like the others."

"How in hell's name did you get them all here. Same as me? Calling in markers I suppose."

"And making a few promises I hope I'll be able to keep."

"So what do you do now?"

"To be honest I'm not sure. I've several options, among which is to do fuck all . . ."

"Can't see you adopting that course of action."

"Nor can I, but maybe I'll be forced to. We've had a lot of pressure already. But in any event, I'm still waiting for the report from the intelligence boys. I'll make my final decision when I have that."

"Good luck."

The doc took a last look at the never-ending rows of young dead, and made for his Land Rover. A Russian laborer who crossed his path saw his expression and shrank back.

Revell had already sensed how uptight everyone was. Anger had added an air of menace to every order the NATO troops gave members of the Russian labor battalion. In their turn the deserters were becoming nervous and edgy, as the realization dawned of what a tightrope they walked.

They kept their heads down, avoiding eye contact, and working hard enough to bring little extra attention to themselves. Their main task now was the clearing of a tract of virgin land and the preparation of one hundred and ninety two individual graves. Others prepared the plain wooden crosses for each. Even Grigori worked, trying to blend in among the others.

Watching them was an alert circle of troops with fingers on the triggers of their rifles. There had been no incidents so far, but Revell was all too well aware that a trivial act could bring one about at any moment.

The arrival of the nurses had helped calm things a little. Working in teams of three they had begun washing the bodies, and wrapping them in clean white sheets.

Men of the combat company kept them supplied with water from the tanker, and soap, sheets and body bags from the stores truck parked beside it.

The elderly officer of the West German army's service corp who had arrived with them, had already volunteered himself and his drivers to join in any action Revell might take.

That accounted for four of the six couriers he had sent out. It would be midday tomorrow, Friday, before he would know if the other two had been as successful. If they hadn't been, then all this would have been for nothing.

Well, not quite for nothing. He stood to the side and observed as the nurses finished washing dirt and blood from yet another young victim. It was a girl, very thin, and as white as the neatly folded sheet beside her. Hair brushed back from her face, she looked no more than eight or nine. Her arms and legs flopped about like those of a disjointed rag doll when she was lifted for the wrapping to pass under her emaciated body.

Very gently the crisp material was enfolded about her, after a generous dusting with a sickly sweet smelling disinfectant powder. Then again she was lifted and placed into a body bag. She made a pitifully small load within it.

"A terrible business, Major. A truly terrible business."

The middle-aged chaplain who had come out with the nurses had been constantly trotting back and forth between the scene of preparation and the graves. He looked and sounded exhausted, both mentally and physically, but it was as though he couldn't stop.

"Some of the men have said they would like to speak with me. Under no circumstances I wonder if that would be in order."

"I have never stopped my men from attending a church parade if they want, even though we don't hold them ourselves. Certainly they can talk to you."

"You misunderstand, Major. I have spoken to several of your men and to a number of the Dutch pioneers already. No, I have been approached by one of the Russians . . ."

"Grigori, by any chance?"

"Yes, that was his name. When they have finished their work, they would like a service. I can well understand that feeling is running high, but they are not the men who . . . who did this terrible crime."

There was a horrendous scream, or the start of one, from the direction of the improvised graveyard. Revell had hardly started toward it when Hyde approached.

"That was one of the Russians. The silly bastard got a mouth full of dirt and spat it out into one of the graves. Old William swung a shovel at him."

"How bad is he?"

Hyde glanced at the chaplain. "They don't come any worse. It took his head clean off."

Chapter 19

Revell had only been studying the electronic intelligence data for a few minutes when the Military Police arrived.

"There's a general who would like to see you, Major. And I think he'll be wanting those as well."

"Help yourself." Revell made no further comment as the print-outs, photographs and typed sheets were gathered together.

"Am I under arrest."

Both the MPs were sergeants, and both were big, seeming to fill the interior of the tent. It was the older of the two, the one with several medal ribbons who spoke again.

"Those aren't our orders, Major, but the general gave us his instructions in person. You could say he was not happy. I haven't ever been spoken to by a general before. If they all get as mad as he was, I'm content for it to never happen again." He shuffled the papers together. "Are there any copies of these?"

"Here? No."

The MPs exchanged looks. Again it was the veteran

who spoke. "I would like to be able to take the word of an officer, Major. But if I go back and tell the general I accepted that then he is quite likely to nail my balls to my kneecaps. We'll have a look around."

The search of the tent and its sparse furnishings took only a moment, but it was done thoroughly. Outside a third MP waited by a highly polished Hummer. He had his hand close to his holster and had unbuttoned the covering flap.

As Revell was escorted to the waiting transport a growing crowd of his men encircled it and a threatening rumble of noise came from them.

"Tell your men to keep back, Major. We're just doing our job."

It was obvious the MPs were nervous. Tall and wide as they were, Dooley was more than their match when he planted himself in their path. He fixed them with a glare that was almost hypnotic in its intensity.

"Move over, Dooley. That's an order." For a second Revell thought he was going to disobey, but begrudgingly he stepped back among the throng.

During the brief delay the young MP had been looking through the photographs, concentrating on one that showed a long line of children's bodies.

"Have you guys been killing babies?"

The fist that hit him in the side of the face came from the second rank of the crowd, but for all the distance it had to travel, it came with crushing force.

A bone cracked loudly and following the impact of the blow the MP went down, bouncing with a heavy thud off the hood of the Hummer. He slid to the ground, eyes rolling, jaw hanging limp. Blood spurted from the back of his throat.

"That's enough." Revell had to shout.

Both standing MPs had their pistols out, with safety catches off. In reply to that action came the distinctive click of a round being chambered in an M16. The circle about the group tightened.

"It's OK. I'll be back. I'll be back soon." Revell had to think fast to do something to defuse the situation.

Before he could say more he was bundled into the back of the Hummer. He had to slide across when the semi-conscious MP was shoved in beside him.

"They broke my buddy's jaw."

The big sergeant climbed into the driver's seat. He sent the vehicle surging forward. Its fenders brushed those slowest to get out of the way.

"You ain't the only one who'll be coming back, Major. Difference is, I won't be on my own."

"What the hell are you playing at out there. Don't orders mean anything to you?"

Revell held his tongue. The general had worked himself into a fine old lather and wasn't about to allow interruptions.

"I'll bet you've got some smart ass explanation about how you thought the order didn't cover a second mass grave. Well I'm telling you, you can be as big a smart ass as you fancy, you're not talking your way out of this one."

Stalking back and forth across the room, the general opened his mouth to speak several times, but couldn't find the words. Finally he turned to Colonel Lippincott.

"He's your damned subordinate. Don't you have any

control over your men? Can't you impose any discipline? Do you have any idea who I've had on the phone in the last hour? I'll tell you. Two damned politicians and a lieutenant general from the staff at Army Headquarters. He has the army commander's ear. God only knows what sort of influence the other two can swing."

"I've spoken to the major." Lippincott took advantage of a pause to jump in. "He does feel that the discovery of the second mass burial changes the situation. Using his own discretion he thought it wise to make a record."

Revell experienced quiet amazement. It was the first time, ever, that he had heard Ol' Foul Mouth get through a sentence without injecting an obscenity.

"And what damned good did he think that would do?" Grabbing a handful of the reports and photographs, the general waved them. "Have you seen these?"

"I have examined them, General. I can understand how Major Revell . . ."

"You understand, horseshit."

Lippincott expanded visibly as he changed color. "Would the general like to elaborate."

Now pacing the floor behind his desk, the general appeared to have already forgotten what he'd said in anger. He was so worked up that his breath was coming in snorts. His fists clenched and unclenched repeatedly. He stopped behind his chair, put his hands on the back of it and looked hard at them.

"When I finish here I've got to go to a meeting to discuss this whole damned messy business. Among other things they'll want to know how a lowly major could be able to put together an intelligence file inches thick inside of twelve hours. And they're especially going to want to find out how he commandeered those resources, after he'd been told to keep his damned nose out of the matter."

Picking up a battered briefcase, the general began to cram the assorted documents into it. "To keep the lid on this we've had to round up all your fellow conspirators. If we hadn't moved fast when we found what was going on, by now every cook and bottle washer in the Zone would be in on it. You can't begin to imagine how much time and effort it has taken." With an effort the general brought his temper under control.

"You think you've been smart, Major. I'll bet you've a duplicate set tucked away somewhere. Well, I'm not about to be blackmailed. I swear to you that the best you can hope for from now on is to remain a major until you're the oldest one in any army in the Zone. Get out."

Revell saluted, and went to reach for the door. He was pulled up by another outburst.

"If the games you've been playing make half the trouble for me that I'm expecting, then I'll make sure you go in the shit with me. And you know what? When we're both buried in it, I'll be standing on your head."

The outer room was spartanly furnished, with a selection of odd chairs. It looked like a doctor's waiting room belonging to a poor practice in a poorer area. Once it must have been the principal bedroom of the big old house that was the HQ. Fancy plasterwork decorated the ceiling, and the threadbare carpet had once been a good one.

There was one other person in there, a captain who looked much too old for his rank, and ill at ease in his crumpled uniform. Revell didn't recognize the insignia he wore.

"Seems to be a lot of shouting in there. But then I've found there's a lot of that in the army. My name's Porter. I suppose I should say 'captain' first, but I can't get used to it."

At first glance Revell had summed the officer up as a civilian in uniform. He didn't feel much like making small talk, but anything was better than having to listen to the muted, unintelligible bellowing coming from next door.

"Revell. Not sure what rank I should say. Not sure what it'll be tomorrow."

"Oh, I see. All that racket is aimed directly, or presently indirectly, at you. What have you done, anything absolutely outrageous?"

"What branch are you with? I don't recognize the badge."

"Hardly surprising. I shouldn't think there are many of us. I'm with the historical section of the War Department. We are supposed to trot about the battlefields recording events for posterity. Only I shouldn't be doing it. That's why I was hoping to see the general."

"What should you be doing?" The scruffy officer amused Revell, and he could do with light relief. Never before had he ever seen a soldier so obviously lacking any shadow of a martial spirit.

"Actually, until I was drafted," Porter winced as another indistinct blast of noise came through the wall, "I was a school teacher."

"History?"

"Among everything else, certainly, but I'm no historian. And I can't go trekking across battlefields interviewing marines and soldiers. I don't know where to start. Apart from anything else, I'm too old. It's a task that needs a younger, fitter man. Now if I had been sent out here as a reporter . . ."

A look of dreamy bliss came over the captain's placid features. "That's what I always wanted to be. I could see myself, my own desk at the *Tribune* or the *Post,* getting all the scoops. Actually I do manage a little in that way. I send in local stories to our county paper. Some get into print. Rewritten usually of course, but now and again I get a byline."

In the adjoining room the shouting appeared to have reached and then passed the crisis point. The door burst open and the general, red in the face, stamped past Revell and the captain without giving either a glance.

Half rising from his seat, Porter couldn't summon the courage to call after him, and slumped back down.

"Major Revell!"

Anticipating the colonel's summons, Revell had already started for the office. He turned back to Porter. The man seemed entirely crushed, drained. "Keep trying. Today is just a bad day. Perhaps you'll get in the press corps yet."

"I shan't hold my breath. I would like to think it could happen, but do you know, I truly believe that if a scoop . . . if a scoop sat in the same room, I wouldn't recognize it."

"Perhaps you're right." Walking into the office, Revell pulled the door shut behind him, and faced the colonel.

Chapter 20

"Did you keep a duplicate set?"

Lippincott had plunked himself in the general's swivel chair. Now he helped himself to a substantial pinch of the general's pipe tobacco. He sniffed the mixture, grunted disparagingly and put it back in its stained leather pouch.

He idly opened each desk drawer in turn as he spoke. "Or is there more than one lot of copies?"

"There is another complete record, including an expertly shot three hour video."

"Clever bastard, aren't you. I suppose if we send the MPs back they won't find anything."

"Can't be sure, I would think it highly unlikely."

In a sliding tray immediately below the rear of the desk top, Lippincott found a tray of assorted pencil stubs.

"Look at this. You can tell a lot about a man by the way he looks after his pencils. Not a decent point on any of them. Very sloppy."

Rummaging at the back of the tray Lippincott finally found a fresh pencil. "Good, 2H. I find HB's have no flavor."

"So what happens now. Do I go back to my combat company?"

"Not so fast, Major. At this precise moment you are getting a severe reprimand." Looking around, Lippincott finally spat a sliver of gold letter embossed green paint into a waste-paper basket. "Consider yourself fucking lucky. Only one thing preventing them from putting you under close arrest, prior to a full court martial and the inevitable kicking of your ass all the way to the stockade."

"The copies?"

"No, not your shitty copies. Having those is what nearly sank you for good. That was too tricky for the general to stomach. Too damned clever by half. What saved your miserable bacon was a memo from the eggheads in public relations."

"They've never done anything helpful or useful before. Who woke them up, somebody offering free drinks?"

"Don't despise them, Major. It's those drunken lard asses who pulled you out of the fire. Almost out, that is. They have to think ahead, anticipate, you might say. Their thinking is that, despite all our efforts, this business might just, eventually, make the papers. We're fighting tooth and nail to put a block on that, but . . . Well, how's it going to look if the hero who uncovered the story has been busted and is doing ten."

Sick of the whole business, with its double talk and the double standards that went with it, Revell simply wanted to get back to his company. After all this, the Zone appeared almost an attractive alternative.

"So everything goes back to normal. Like nothing

has happened."

"That's it, business as usual." Pulling a face, Lippincott threw the half-eaten pencil into the basket. "Tastes like chipboard. Can't even requisition himself decent pencils. Yeah, as long as we can keep the lid on the story, there's no harm done."

"Except to a couple of thousand West German civvies and their kids. The lid was put on them all right."

"Major, you can be a real tit. You think you're the only one with feelings. I feel for them, even me, Ol' Foul Mouth. In private the general does as well. He's as mad about it as you and me. Maybe more, because he never gets out on the ground, knows he'll never be able to throttle the fuckers with his bare hands as he'd like to. He has to be part of the cover-up operation, so he takes it out on us. Tough for us, but perfectly natural, you have to agree."

"So the KGB get away with another one. Only this time we help them get away with it."

"Hand me my attache case case will you?" Lippincott accepted it, and delved inside. From it he extracted a large thermos flask, a couple of Mars bars and a large bundle of pencils. He piled them all on the desk top. "Here it is."

Pulling out a thick file, he tossed it to Revell. "It's not what you would call light reading. Not in any sense of the word."

Opening it, Revell read the title page to himself. "This a complete intelligence summary on the 717th. Why give me it, rubbing salt in the wounds?"

"Hardly, and you take good care of that, soon as you've finished reading it in fact." Pushing the items back into the case, Lippincott kept the pencils until last, popping two into his pocket.

"That was put together for me by a friendly, if rather matronly type, in records. She has the hots for me. Yeah, I know what you're thinking, but it's not just you glamorous types who can get your end away. You'll be grateful for the likes of her if you get turned into a one-armed wonder like me." Lippincott had seen Revell's quiet smile. "Just don't you go getting sloppy when you dispose of that. It wouldn't be so difficult to trace. The old photocopier in the filing room produces blemishes as distinctive as any fingerprint."

"So why are you taking the risk." While he listened Revell couldn't resist flicking over the pages in his lap. From that brief survey it appeared a mine of information.

"Because I get this gut feeling when you're up to something. I reckon, regardless of the consequences, you and your crazy outfit are going to hit the 717th. For you to stand half a chance of pulling it off, cleanly, you need all the assistance you can get. This is the best I can do, toward avoiding being pulled down with you if it all goes wrong. Can you use it?"

"There's certainly good stuff in here. Strengths, equipment scales; even profiles on their CO and his officers."

"You are going to raid them, aren't you?"

Until that precise moment, Revell had not made up his mind. He looked directly at the colonel. "Yes." There was nothing to be gained by a denial.

"Shit, you haven't even got the decency to be evasive, have you. No wonder those politicians hated you. I just hope to God you know what you're doing. Screw up this truce and you'll be responsible for so many deaths that the best efforts by the KGB are going to look like chicken shit. That'll make you no better than one of them. You want that label, that sort of responsibility?"

"I have to accept it. I couldn't live with myself if I didn't try to do something."

"You try, and screw up, and you won't want to live with yourself."

"I know that." Just saying the words made Revell feel cold and hollow inside. Even now he was still trying hard to justify, to himself, what he was about to do. "Once the truce breaks though, that bunch of Warpac child killers could end up anywhere. Or the unit might be broken up to make reinforcements. This will be the only chance."

Starting on a fresh pencil, Lippincott stayed quiet and sunk in thought for a while. "I can't back you on this, you know that. The strings that would need pulling to protect you, if you survive, are way out of my reach. Shit, I wish I were going with you. How many . . . no, don't tell me. What I don't know I can't damned well worry over. Go on, get out before I pull back that file, come back to my senses and blow the whistle on you."

Revell hadn't expected it, but the colonel replied to his salute. He was almost out the door when Lippincott called after him.

"That bodybag in my chopper. I thought my pilot was doing a spot of smuggling, had a look inside. Was that the guy who showed up on the aerial shot?"

Revell turned and nodded.

"Figures. You were bringing a body home. Nice touch. Maybe your outfit ain't all bad."

"They're what the Zone has made them."

Closing the door, Revell went out through the waiting room. Captain Porter was still there, but didn't notice the major. He was leaned back on his chair, a faint smile on his face, in a trance.

He was a few thousand miles away, at a features desk, handling one great scoop after another. His imagination was filled with front pages, headlines and bylines, but most of all with scoops. Not that he would have recognized one if it had been in the same room.

Chapter 21

In precisely four hours they would commence phase two. Twenty minutes after that, they would be irretrievably committed. Until that moment they could still abort. They could hope to hook back the advance elements without being detected, and prevent an incident.

For the hundredth time Revell compared the sand-table model with the photographs supplied by the Royal Artillery's RPV. The remotely piloted miniature helicopter's cameras had done a beautiful job. The low-high-low flight profile appeared to have got it over the enemy position without being noticed. From a thousand feet, the ten frames it had taken had encompassed the whole area.

On the table, held in place by impaling twigs, scraps of paper marked the positions of buildings. The farm was an old one, with a mix of half timbered and metal clad structures. Work already begun indicated that it would eventually become a formidable defensive position. And that work was proceeding at a rapid pace.

If the work of fortifying it had only begun a few days

previously, and evidence such as the obviously freshly turned earth indicated that was the case, then in a week or less it would have become virtually impregnable to all but a full-scale assault.

A red stain was spreading across the carefully sculpted material on the table. It was a reminder of its previous use and, as if any were needed, of why they were making their preparations.

They'd cross the start line as well-briefed as they ever had been on any mission. Revell's principal concern was the severe limitation on the number of men he could take. Those he employed would have to do a lot of damage in a very short time. To do that, they would have to be armed to the teeth. And to survive to exploit that massive firepower they would have to move fast, and keep moving.

The farm stood in isolation, at the center of a patchwork of overgrown fields. After leaving the cover of the woods, the road ran dead straight for a kilometer. It would be impossible for their approach to escape detection. They would be under observation from the moment they left cover.

Close by, the pioneers were working hard to get their transport ready. It said a lot for the seriousness of their task that they did not find the humor in the situation that they otherwise would have done.

"How's this, Major?" Burke held out a bucket for its contents to be inspected.

"Touch more white should do it."

Burke trudged away, muttering.

Revell leafed through the transcripts of communication intercepts. The translation of an outgoing ordnance requisition was particularly revealing. Taken at face value it indicated that the 717th had very little in the way of mines or anti-tank weapons. It would be dangerous to let that belief lull him into a false sense of security.

The electronic survey had indicated that they were not employing any form of automated perimeter alarms. But that wasn't proof that they didn't have them. Such equipment might be temporarily down for repair or maintenance. Taken together the reports indicated almost a mirror of the situation that had very likely existed here. Plenty of physical barriers, a complex network of defenses but little accompanying sophistication. No intruder alarms, no off road mines, no radars of any description.

An analysis of traffic movements and vehicle types tended to confirm a picture of a poorly equipped unit, with almost unlimited labor available for hardening the position.

Traffic during the twelve hours of monitoring had been exceptionally light, even for a Soviet infantry outfit. Only four-cylinder motors had been detected, and those unshielded. That meant no armor. The danger that some might be parked up due to shortage of fuel had been discounted by the RPV photographs.

It was tempting to delay the attack until Sunday or Monday, but Revell had a feeling that it had to be Saturday. It had meant a tremendous last-minute rush as the last of the couriers had only returned in the small hours.

He looked again at the photograph that concerned him most, and had prompted his decision to go in immediately. Among all the other works going on, one was very distinctive.

The posts and wire of the large compound were barely visible, except under magnification. That was not the case with the wooden watch towers under construction at each corner.

From that, Revell looked again at the file Colonel Lippincott had supplied. The profile on Tarkovski was like reading a biography of a composite Capo, Jack the Ripper and deSade. Apparently this was his third spell with the 717th; his first as its commander. Did that indicate that he was crafty enough to avoid the death penalty three times, or nasty enough to ensure that there was always employment for his ugly talents? On reflection Revell thought it likely a blend of both qualities.

He checked his watch. Clarence would be in position by now. His escort would be back fairly soon. Left out in his isolated position the sniper had an unenviable task but one suited well to his particular skills.

"We're ready to start painting, Major. You want to have a look?"

About to follow Hyde, Revell paused. Going to the field kitchen, he flicked open the door, and thrust the thick file into the fire.

"How would you like it done." Scully, reclosing it, put his hand on the draught regulator.

"Well done. In fact I don't want anything left."

Behind him he heard the flames grow fierce. It wouldn't be that easy to dispose of the real thing.

"Couldn't fit on even one more. Not anywhere." Burke stood back from the eight-wheeled Soviet APC.

Every inch of its steeply raked hull was adorned with

the angular outline of reactive armor boxes. Sandbags had been rammed into the gap between the trim board and the glacis plate. On its roof, to conceal the machine gun that had been positioned in the turret, a clutter of easily jettisonable cases and parcels had been apparently carelessly stacked.

The second BTR 70 had been treated in similar fashion, with the exception that after removal of the blanking plate from the turret, a grenade launcher had been emplaced.

"I've always thought of myself as having an artistic streak." Garrett plunged a large paint brush into the bucket, drew it out dripping with paint and began to slap the pink concoction over the armor's additions.

"What a bloody way to go to war. In a mobile whore house, and a pink one at that." Hyde stepped back to stay out of range of the splashes.

"Can you think of any other way we can get into the KGB camp without getting shot to ribbons." Ackerman dunked a large sponge into the container and began to daub the vehicle's flank. "It was very good of Frau Lilly to let us have these."

"At a price." Hyde took a further step away.

"That's as may be. She could still have sold them as a business proposition. These are her trademark. Once we've used them for this, that's it. Anyway, Sarge, the seats in there are a lot more comfortable than the usual benches."

Hyde snorted and left the decorators to their work. Soon they would start loading fuel and ammunition. That would be his principal contribution to the preparations. The revised crew compartment, furbished more with the comfort of the girls in mind than practical fighting qualities, presented problems.

The usual crew for the vehicle would be driver and commander, plus sixteen infantry passengers. Due to the quantity of weapons and munitions to be carried they would be reducing that to a total of twelve.

Watching the work in progress, Lieutenant Vokes prowled back and forth, appearing to want to say something; finally he went up to the major.

"My men, myself included, would like to come with you, Major."

"Can't be done. We'll be pushing our luck by including a third vehicle. Any more and they're likely to be suspicious. To get close we have to get them completely off their guard. Arriving mob handed won't work. No point in improving the odds if we never get the chance to employ them. Is that project of yours finished yet?"

"Almost. We are enclosing the load in a mound of flak-jackets, as protection from small arms and splinters, but there is little else we can do. The driver will be very vulnerable."

"It'll have to do. When the time comes we'll lift your ambush party to their positions by shoving them on top."

"I wish I were coming with you, instead of remaining here."

"You might end up being very glad you stayed. This is no party we're going to."

Chapter 22

The sniper's body ached all over, especially his wrists. His elbows felt as though they must be red-raw. After working solidly for three hours he was at last satisfied with his concealment, and allowed himself a short rest.

In the shallow, turf-roofed, trench he had to turn partially on his side to take a sip from his water bottle. It tasted flat and tepid, heavily tainted with a flavor of swimming pools.

Tightly stretched and staked plastic netting supported knife cut squares of grass above him. Fibrous roots showed as a pale intricate network against the dark damp soil. As he wriggled forward on his stomach in the cramped hideout, severed roots of trees stroked his hands and face.

They had made it difficult digging in, but once he had chosen his spot he had to stick with it. There had to be minimum disturbance of the site. False starts and subsequent relocation would increase the chances of detection.

He fractionally widened the opening in the front of

the trench, where it all but broke through into the forward slope of the steep wooded ridge. Through a powerful telescope he examined the KGB encampment.

Smoke drifted sluggishly from a garbage pit. A darker column emerging through the broken roof of an ancient barn indicated the site of the cookhouse. By the front wall of the farmhouse stood a Gaz field car. The building was massively sandbagged, and work appeared still to be going on to further improve its protection. Laid out in a "U" shape around a courtyard that opened toward the road, every window was walled up, and the doors protected by blast walls.

There were a dozen large barns and other buildings in the complex, plus silos and many smaller structures. Taking his time, Clarence made a careful sweep, noting every detail of the farm. Then he panned across the open ground surrounding it.

Freshly turned earth betrayed the positions of trenches and gun pits. Some of the excavations had overhead cover in the shape of improvised camouflage or rough logs. None appeared to be manned, or to have any weapons emplaced.

Focusing back on the main house, he examined the roof. Apart from a few missing tiles, it was largely intact. It was the flat roof of an extension that drew his attention.

In deep shadow in the photograph he had studied, at the well-lit shallow angle from which he viewed it now, there was no mistake. Surrounded by a low parapet of plump sandbags, lavishly draped with netting, was a twin cannon mount.

At the distance it was not possible for Clarence to

positively identify the weapon, but whether 23 or 30mm, it made little difference. Either was lethal against the targets that would shortly be presenting themselves. Set for a dual purpose ground and anti-aircraft role, the cannon's field of fire was every inch of the approach route from the woods.

Recapping the telescope lens, the sniper edged back to the center of the trench. From his pack he extracted a short thick section of planking. Positioning it so that two studs set in it were uppermost, he pounded it into the already compacted soil with his fist. Next he reached behind him and dragged forward the long and awkward bulk of his Barrett fifty-caliber rifle. Weighing upward of thirty pounds, it was strenuous work in the confined space and by the time its five feet of length were in position he was sweating profusely.

Setting the drilled-out feet of its bipod on the studs, Clarence carefully unwrapped the weapon's ten-power sighting telescope and scanned the enemy camp again.

Although only inches wide, the aperture in the sparse turf of the forward slope gave him an excellent field of vision at two thousand yards range. Satisfied, he redraped the scope, and placed beside the trigger group a satchel of pre-loaded eleven round magazines.

A thought struck him, and he uncovered the telescopic sight once more. Examining the twin mount on the flat roof, he panned back and forth across it, making fractional adjustments as he did.

Patiently he kept the weapon in view. He didn't have long to wait. From an angle of the roof a shirtless Warpac soldier strolled to the edge of the roof and unbuttoned himself. He stood there for several seconds before bothering to look over.

It was unlikely he would have completed the function in so casual a fashion if he had known that at that moment a sniper rifle telescopic sight was focused on him.

"One hour." Ripper checked his watch for the fifth time in as many minutes.

"So we all know what the time is, great. Could you quit the countdown." Carrington dealt yet another hand of poker.

Picking up his cards, Dooley rolled his eyes to heaven. "I'm out." He threw the cards down. "Why should I be the only one who never gets any of those with the pretty pictures on the front."

"Hang around." Hyde fanned his hand in compact fashion, making no expression. His face was incapable of any. "You'll be seeing something as pretty as a picture soon enough."

"How come?" Clutching his cards in untidy fashion, Garrett kept switching them about. "Did Ackerman smuggle one of those whores back here."

"Wash your fucking mouth with soap. You mind how you talk about them or I'll smash it in." Dooley glared, but didn't follow up the threat.

"I was only saying . . ."

"Shut up, Garrett. Are you playing?"

He looked at the sergeant, then hurriedly away. The man's disfigurement gave him the creeps. "I can't concentrate with all this talking going on. I'm out as well."

"This is no bloody fun at all." Carrington gave Hyde the two he asked for, took three for himself. He barely glanced at them, before tossing the greasy cards into the center of the blanket.

"It's all yours, Sarge. You might as well take it. You've got my pay for the next three weeks, might as well make it the whole month. Anyway, what is all this about the possibility of female company?"

"It's already here. You'll see her in a minute."

"Oh yeah." Wistfully, Ripper watched his money being raked in. "And what sort of crazy dame is going to be out here at this time?"

"The trouble with you lot is that you can't see what's right under your noses."

"Come on, Sarge." Ripper's voice was loudest among the chorus of complaint. "Let's have it, come on, spill the beans."

"If you're going to be that impatient, I'll give you all a clue."

"Aw crap. Now we play guessing games."

In his turn, Dooley was shouted down by the others.

"What is it we're employing as a sort of Trojan Horse . . ."

"What's a trojan . . ."

It was Garrett's turn to be bellowed into silence.

"It's a mobile whore house, isn't it?" Hyde noticed that Dooley appeared to be about to voice further indignation and annoyance, and went on quickly. "Now everyone in the Zone knows about Frau Lilly's outfit. Even if they've never seen it, they'll have heard all about it. But anyone can respray a couple of old Soviet armored personnel carriers, and then try pulling a few stunts. The wonder is that no one appears to have done it so far . . ."

"That's as well," Ripper grinned, "else her girls would have started getting a different welcome from the one they're used to."

A muted rumbling noise came from Dooley, but he saw the NCO was watching him, and thought better of it.

"If I can go on?" Hyde finished shuffling the notes into neat stacks. He began to pocket them, with tantalizing slowness and deliberation.

"Maybe the nasty piece of work who bosses the 717th is twisted enough to think on those lines. Could be he'd shoot first, ask questions after, if he did at all. So we needed an ace . . ."

"You don't. I reckon you print your own, the number you get dealt . . ."

This time there was no shouting, but Ripper felt all eyes on him. His words petered out.

"And talk of the devil, she's here." Hyde made a show of looking over Dooley's head, toward the trees, and the others turned to look.

Silence. Not a word, not a whistle. No grunts, no catcalls, no dirty laughs or smutty remarks. Silence.

"What is the matter. Have you not seen a woman before?"

Before any of them could articulate a single word, Andrea was gone. It was Garrett who broke the silence. "Shit, I've never seen her dressed like that before, you know, like a female."

"I've never seen her sober before," Carrington added.

Ripper groaned. "I've never suffered from premature ejaculation before."

"You what?" Dooley finally managed to screw his head back into its more usual position on his neck. He had followed Andrea from sight without moving his body, through almost a complete circle. "What's that?"

"I've come in my pants."

"Rather there than in mine." Carrington gently rippled the deck, thoughtfully. "That was cleavage I saw. I know it was. I've never thought of her as having tits."

"I think on the basis of what we've just seen it's safe to assume, that in every respect, Andrea is all woman." Along the boundary wire of the Russian compound, Hyde noticed the prisoners were standing three deep. The card players had not comprised her only appreciative audience.

"Will this do?" Turning on her toes, Andrea displayed the tight stretch jeans and low cut top. Her dark hair, combed out and shining, swung across her face and accentuated her high cheeks and deep brown eyes.

"Yes, yes that's fine. It's fine." That had to be the greatest understatement Revell had ever spoken.

She had been unkempt and bleary eyed from drink for so long, he'd almost forgotten how attractive . . . no, how beautiful she really was.

The transformation was truly incredible. It was only when he looked harder, and closer, that he could still see traces of the puffy face and blood-shot eyes. They had been concealed by the surprisingly skilful application of make-up.

"You know I would not have done this, had there been any other way you would have included me in on the raid."

For a brief moment Revell had been wishing things back the way they were, the way they had been when he had first known her. Then he'd worshiped her, had been totally devoted to her. But gradually her indifference had beaten those feelings out of him. And here, once more, she was sweeping away any chance of their revival.

"And you know you're only in because your presence tilts the scales a little in our favor." He would have given much to cut her down to size, but she was impervious to any sarcasm he could summon. "So do your job when the time comes. Until then I don't want to see you."

Chapter 23

The clothes, like the cosmetics and her unrestrained hair, felt strange. Andrea walked among the trees, putting distance between herself and Revell. Between herself and all of them.

She tolerated their oafish company, or had so far, because with them there was always ample opportunity for killing. That was changing though. This raid could be the last before the combat company was disbanded.

Before that happened, before NATO Field Intelligence got their hands on her and put her in the cage reserved for ex-East German border guards, she would disappear. There were plenty of opportunities to join other, less official units fighting in the giant no-man's-land of the Zone.

Perhaps she would start her own gang again. Men were so easy to control. As long as they were led to believe they were in charge they could be manipulated effortlessly. And they never realized.

What would Major Revell do? He had kept the command together through more than fifty actions;

rebuilt it when their numbers had been reduced to that of a handful of wounded survivors. For most of her time with him the unit had operated almost like one of the old free-companies.

Starved of weapons and vehicles, by an HQ that didn't approve of what it saw as the diluting effect of so-called private armies, it had kept itself supplied by taking what it wanted. Battlefield salvage, capture from the enemy and outright theft from their own dumps; that was how it had survived.

From each of the best men she had plucked different skills. That of the sniper from Clarence, the subtle techniques of command from Revell, combat driving from Burke. And much more, from many others.

She had fought off passes and outright attempts at rape. And been successful. Dooley's instruction in unarmed fighting had been an important factor in that.

Looking down she saw the swell of her breasts above the flimsy ruffles of the whore's blouse. Ackerman had obtained it for her. The only part of the outfit she liked was the black leather boots. High heeled, they were tight fitting to the knee.

Stupid women. Resorting to such things, and for what? In the case of the prostitute whose clothes she wore, so that she could get a man to make money, so that she could go out and get a man. It was pathetic, futile.

Between her legs she felt the seam of the jeans rubbing into her. She looked about to see that she was alone. The woods were still. There was no sound. Leaning back against a tree she ran her hands from her throat, over her breasts, across her flat stomach to the tops of her thighs.

A drink. She'd have given anything for a drink. But those had been Revell's terms. One drink, no raid. The major knew she would not take one, but he couldn't stop her thinking. Swallowing hard, she tried to push the thought from her.

The action of unfastening her narrow leather belt was almost an unconscious one, as was the moving of her hands to her waistband. Edging the jeans from side to side as she eased them down over her hips, she closed her eyes. Very gently she slid her hand underneath her body and began gently to rub. At the first contact she was wet, and her fingers slid inside.

Her mind was cluttered with thoughts that she didn't want. She thought of those stupid whores. All women were stupid, but at least they were usually clean, not covered in hair with those ugly stupid things between their legs. What of the whore who had worn this blouse. She would do anything for money, anything. Even do this, if she were given enough.

Andrea's fingers moved more urgently. Yes, even this.

The only difference to the scene laid out before the sniper's position was the gradual lengthening of the shadows. He could see only a small arc of the sky, above the distant horizon. It was free of cloud, and he hoped it would continue that way.

He had checked very carefully before determining on this precise location for his hideout. The sun would set directly behind him.

That was where it would be when he opened fire. Any special sighting device used in an attempt to spot his muzzle flashes would be hopeless, swamped by the flare of the sun's disc.

There had been occasions recently when he had wondered if there was any point in continuing to try to evade what he knew to be inevitable.

The odds against his continuing survival were lengthening dramatically with every day and every action in which he took part. He was already a statistical absurdity. He was but a few short of a kill total of three hundred. And those were the ones of which he could be as close to a hundred percent certain as was possible.

A sniper rarely saw, close-up, the results of his work. Even when much of it was done at ranges of a couple of hundred yards or less. But when a bullet struck, men reacted in different ways. A hit in a limb usually produced a dramatic reaction from the target. A good solid strike in the torso or head was very different. It was like the air had suddenly been exhausted from a blow-up doll. They collapsed as if instantly deflated.

At the closer ranges he often saw his victim's face before, at or even immediately after impact. If it was a head shot their cranium would explode a shower of blood and bone and brain tissue. The change of expression was always instantaneous. He never recalled specific instances, only had in mind a softly focused montage. There were never any dreams, but then he hardly ever slept, and only then when so tired he could not avoid its necessity.

The time was passing steadily; it never troubled him, the waiting. There had been a time, in the weeks after the stalling of the first Russian attacks, when he had waited literally days for a single target. These few hours were nothing by comparison.

There was one thought, pushed deep into the innermost recesses of his mind, that he was not ready to deal with. It had surfaced from time to time, but always been subdued once more, shunted into a cobwebby corner.

With his tally standing where it did, it was becoming harder to do that. This was the day he would fulfill his vow. The one he had made at the graveside of his wife and children. What a long time ago that seemed.

Then he had thought this a moment to look forward to, a time for laying down his burden and joining them. The realization struck him that he, a man who had handed out death hundreds of times, was afraid of it himself.

The interior of the APC was packed with weapons and ammunition. Hyde dropped in through a roof hatch and threaded his way forward. The fancy interior still smelled of perfume, but the crushed velvet seat covers were marked by dust and oil, and all the cushions had been thrown out. He sat in the commander's chair, and let his body go limp.

Thirty minutes before the off. In this unit it was unusual to go into action with a specific start time. In getting everything ready it had been a help, given them targets to achieve. In preparing them for what lay ahead he wasn't so sure.

He would have paced the loading, left them with only a few minutes to stand about. All the men wanted to see the job done, see the enemy battalion smashed hard, but they knew the possible consequences when they hit the KGB outfit. The consequences for those of them who returned were more certain. At the very least the command would be broken up.

For individuals the outlook was uncertain. A court-martial for Revell, possibly for Vokes and himself as well. For the others an assortment of dead-end or dangerous assignments. All of them would remain in the Zone. Getting out was a reward, not a punishment.

Except perhaps for him. In the Zone he was just another mutilated victim. Out in the world beyond he would be a freak. After so many years in the army it was hard for him to imagine any other life. But then, when he'd joined the combat company it had been hard to adjust to the free and easy atmosphere, after years of regimental life in a regular unit.

There was a noise behind him. Andrea had climbed in. Ignoring him, she checked through the number of M16 magazines by what would be her position.

Once the action started there would be no time to fumble about looking for things. Clips, grenades and satchel charges would have to come easily to hand.

Andrea finished her inventory and sat down at the far end of the fighting compartment. They said nothing, hardly glanced at each other. Each of them was waiting for the minutes to pass. Waiting for the others to join them, the motors to start. And the killing.

Chapter 24

Tarkovski climbed unsteadily onto the flat roof. He had missed several steps on the home-made ladder and had skinned his ankles each time.

"Find out which of our tame refugees made that fucking ladder, and have him shot." Shouting the instruction down to a passing private, Tarkovski almost overbalanced. He had to flail his arms to prevent himself from falling. The open bottle in his pocket spouted vodka over the side of his jacket.

"No, wait." Sitting down heavily, Tarkovski felt at a splinter in his ankle. "If the shit is so damned good at woodwork, have him make a coffin. Tell him it's his own."

"Then do I shoot him, Colonel?"

"What a shit you are, Private. Where's your bloody style. Put him in the coffin and bury him. No need to bother with the shooting."

"What are you monkeys grinning at?"

Tarkovski rounded on the gun crew. Their faces instantly became blank masks, blank sweating masks. The colonel laughed.

"Cheer up, you miserable shits. We're going to have a party." He scanned the road to the east. "Some of our favorite people are coming. Lots of little civilians. That'll be nice, won't it." A hint of menace came into Tarkovski's voice.

"I said that'll be nice, Private Ivan Petrov." He stuck his face into the man's, breathing alcohol fumes all over him.

"Yes, Comrade Colonel. Very nice."

"Do you know, I'll have a better party than I did last time, if you'll do me a little favor."

"Certainly, Comrade Colonel."

"Oh good. Well if you find another plump little beauty like you did before, I would like to taste her before you do. You still have a passion for licking them, haven't you?"

Petrov froze.

"Shy, in front of your friends. Tell me, what happened to that pretty little plump girl. Did you marry her?"

"The colonel is joking."

"The colonel never fucking jokes." Tarkovski bellowed so loudly the man took an involuntary step backward, stumbling on the edge of the sandbag emplacement.

"She, she fell down stairs and broke her neck, Comrade Colonel."

Tarkovski shook his head sadly. "So many of them do, don't they. I tell you what, before it happens again, you bring any little girl you find to me. Not too little, mind, I like them with big udders. Then while you hold her I'll give her a good lick and then I'll watch you do it to her, until she pisses. You'll enjoy that Petrov. I always do."

Tarkovski made his way back down, slipping and falling the last three steps. He picked himself up, and laughed. He looked at the men watching him from the roof, and deliberately pushed the ladder over.

"Hope you don't miss the party. I tell you what, if you do, Petrov, I'll take care of the plump ones and I'll cut out the piece you like and throw it up to you."

Taking out his bottle, he hoisted it in mock salute and staggered inside, trying to stifle a burp. He paused in the doorway, and shouted to a junior sergeant trying to look busy with a clip-board.

"Let me know as soon as the trucks return with those refugees, I mean our guests. This time I want first pick. Oh, I do love a good party."

The three vehicles stopped well within the border of the woods and dropped off the pioneers with their stores. Revell slid down from the roof of the APC with them and walked to the Toyota pick-up.

Carrington wound down the window. "Something the matter, Major?"

"No, everything is running smoothly. Remember to keep in close behind me. We're not supposed to be an army unit so let's not make ourselves conspicuous by imposing convoy discipline. If shooting starts before we get in among them, then abandon this wagon and grab on to the nearest APC. If we do make it, you know what to do."

"Sure do."

Revell went back to the lead APC. Andrea was arranging herself on the roof, sitting with her legs spread wide, one knee drawn up.

Putting her hands under breasts she bounced them up and down. "Will this do, Major?"

"Yes." Revell had to brush past her to reboard, and caught a hint of perfume. He couldn't be sure if it was hers or if it was from inside the APC, which still reeked of it.

The pioneers were already at work, emplacing off-road mines and other automatic devices.

Revell gauged the position of the sun, made calculations as to how long it would be before it touched the surrounding wooded hills. He thought of Clarence. The sniper had been ready and waiting for several hours. He too would be trying to judge the sun's height above the ridges. Inevitably he would be carrying out last checks on checks he had already made.

"OK, mount up. All hatches closed but not locked," Revell looked at Andrea. "Best keep your's open. You might need to take cover quickly if they rumble us."

"I can take care of myself, Major."

He thought of what he had seen in the woods, when he'd followed her, hoping to talk. "I know you can, and do."

"Comrade Colonel. The trucks have returned."

It took Tarkovski several seconds to absorb and understand the announcement. Shit! He hadn't meant to drink so much today.

He leaned over the side of the bed and shoved his fingers down his throat. The stinging bite of the vomit helped bring him around. A flask of water emptied over his head and a gargle with brandy assisted. Dry-ing his face and hair, he went to the door.

"Where the hell are they?" Tarkovski blinked, dazzled by the sun, now very low in the sky. "Am I supposed to play hide and seek?"

"They are over by their compound, Comrade Colonel." The junior sergeant had to keep ducking and weaving to keep in front of the staggering officer.

"What the hell are they doing all the way over there. Is the party to be at their place? And stay still, you shit. Where are you?"

Another stagger disoriented Tarkovski and he turned a complete circle to face the sergeant once more.

"There you are. Stay there. Now, without indulging in any more shadow boxing. Where are the refugees?"

"By their compound, Colonel. They are still aboard their transport."

"Oh brilliant. Watch my lips, you shit. Why are they all the way over there while I am waiting for them here," he raised his voice to a scream, "like a fucking spare prick at a wedding."

"The drivers say they have been aboard all day and they smell . . ."

"You are as much use as a cock on a priest. Stick your nose in there." With a hefty shove he sent the NCO reeling into the farmhouse doorway.

He jumped back out as if propelled by a physical force, retched violently and then puked.

"And you think I'll be bothered by the fucking smell. On the double, get them over here."

"Comrade Colonel, Comrade Colonel!"

"Stop screeching, what's the excitement?"

A battalion cook came racing around the corner of

the building. His paunch wobbled as he ran and his apron flapped tight against his legs. "Coming across the fields Comrade Colonel, it's coming across the fields!"

Unable to get more sense from the man, Tarkovski thrust the cook aside and went out onto the roadway. He was not the first there, and had to elbow his way through a fast-growing crowd to see what was happening.

"Ah, yes. Now this will be much better than a load of stinking skinny civilians." Eyes lit up in happy anticipation, Tarkovski watched the pair of personnel carriers and their accompanying vehicle laboring toward them over the badly potholed asphalt surface.

His men were obviously of the same opinion. The arrival of the closed trucks, packed with the wretched humanity of the camps, had aroused minimal interest, and no enthusiasm. These brightly colored APCs were a different matter entirely. As the little column drove nearer, some of the waiting men were running backward and forward in excitement.

A woman riding on top of the lead transport waved energetically. She got a thunderous response from the fast growing mob milling about in the road.

Tarkovski shook his head, to try to clear it. This was no time to be drunk, well not yet. Why had he started so early, damn it. Although he'd never seen it for himself, he knew of Frau Lilly's traveling brothel by reputation.

It had only a couple of hundred meters to go. The colonel shaded his eyes with his hand. Behind the APCs the sun was low and bright, it made their garish pink paintwork glisten.

Very pretty, very colorful, Tarkovski thought. But there was something nagging at the back of his mind. Fuck the drink. The spirits he'd drunk that day were still clogging his brain. He was trying to grasp the significance of an important fact, but it continued to elude him.

Shit, it couldn't be that important. Tonight they'd have real party, and later on he'd get one of the girls alone. It would have to be one with great big udders. And when he'd got her alone and had what he wanted, he'd get that present for Petrov.

Chapter 25

The mass of men were starting to surge forward, impatient at the APC's slow progress. First to reach it, only yards ahead of the rest, a lieutenant leaped for the side of the moving vehicle. He grabbed hold, then lost it and rolled off. As he went down his uniform glistened brightly.

Tarkovski saw, and his brain made the final connection of what he had been trying to understand.

"The paint is wet, the paint is wet!" Left on his own in the middle of the road, he screamed after his men, now jubilantly crowding about the lead personnel carrier. "Run, get away!"

At least two thirds of his battalion were packing themselves about the eight wheeler. Above their shouting and whistling he couldn't make himself heard or understood.

Mad with frustration and rage he looked to the gun emplacement. The gunners were searching for a way down. He waved them back.

"Petrov, you bastard. Stay where you are, open fire, you shit! Open fire!" Tarkovski tore his hair and whirled to look at the clusters of men now about both of the APCs. The third vehicle seemed to have gone. On the roof the gunners still stood in indecision. At the top of his voice the colonel ranted at them, spittle shooting from his mouth.

"Open up on them. Fire, you shits, fucking well fire!"

The girl stood up, swaying enticingly, then she reached in among the litter of parcels on the roof and tossed two small black objects into the crowd. At the same instant she dropped from sight through the open hatch.

In the crowd there was a confused tangle of movement. Men who had recognized what was thrown panicked to get clear. Others who wanted to see what it was pressed forward and pinned them against the sides of the hull.

Either side of the APC there were eruptions of flame and smoke and blood. An arm spun through the air and screams drowned the sounds of the engines.

Every hatch aboard both transports clanged back and above every one appeared a rifle, grenade launcher or machine gun.

Chunks of flesh jumped from the crowd as bullets smashed into and through them. A mist of blood hung over the scene as the heavier turret-mounted weapons joined in.

Frozen for a moment, the flak gunners grabbed at the netting over their twin-mount and began to roll it back. Petrov was throwing himself into the gunner's seat when his face was pulped and the back of his head blasted away in a single concave bowl of bone.

Tarkovski hardly saw the body that toppled past him to land with a sickening squelch on the cobbles, destroying the last of the skull.

The ladder slipped as he climbed and he had no time for obscenities as he smacked to the ground beside the corpse. Above him there was a drawn out scream and a jet of blood hosed out in a wide arc. A body flopped across the edge of the roof, an arm and leg and several yards of intestines dangling over the side. Blood and filth ran down the wall.

In swift succession came the familiar sounds of armor-piercing rounds punching through metal. Pushing himself to his feet Tarkovski hoped they were striking the slaughtering APCs, but the fire they started was above him as ready-use ammunition was ignited.

Moving steadily forward, the weapons aboard the APCs were hosing non-stop streams of tracer and grenades into every building and corner.

Two men ran for cover behind the field car. The vehicle seemed to jump and disintegrate in front of his eyes as it was hit by several converging streams of automatic fire.

Taking a last look around, Tarkovski could see no fire being returned. Yelling curses, he ran for the farmhouse door. He was no longer drunk. He passed the truck he'd noticed earlier. This time, though, he paid it no attention, assuming it had stalled alongside the building.

A grenade detonated on the cobbles as he threw himself behind the blast wall. There was a searing pain in his leg, and then he was in cover. When he tried to stand the limb collapsed under him, and he experienced the pain afresh. It was broken, he knew without looking.

Dragging himself, he secured the door and then crawled across to the table. It took a strength-sapping effort but he managed to reach up and grasp the holster on top, then collapsed back in agony. Every movement brought new experiences in pain.

A piece of the top of his boot had been driven into the hole in his calf. On the other side of the leg the leather bulged and blood welled sluggishly every time he moved. The large fragment that had struck him had passed almost from one side of the limb to the other. On the way it had snapped the bone, and driven at least a part of it out through the flesh on the far side. That was what was beneath the bulge.

In the farmhouse the sounds of battle were far less distinct. Not that he could call it a battle. It was too one-sided for that. His men had galloped cheerfully, deliriously, happily to their own bloody execution.

There was nothing to be salvaged but his life. He'd kept that this long, he wasn't about to lose it now. He'd cheated the firing squad once, the hangman twice. This could not be any more difficult than that. First he had to find a place to hide.

There had been no resistance. Revell had thought that once he had heard a bullet skim past, but he could have been mistaken, or it could have been a spent round that had ricocheted from one of the metal-clad barns or silos.

Several of the outer buildings were alight. A huge barn was billowing vast quantities of smoke that was fortunately blowing away from them on the light breeze.

The whole area of the road and courtyard resembled a charnel pit. At least two hundred bodies littered the ground. Many of them, victims of grenades or multiple impacts, were flayed or even totally dismembered. Every wheel on the APC was smothered in a red slush.

Blood also spattered the armor. Carrington sprinted from the cover of a silo, his progress slowed when he slipped and rolled through the worst of the mess. He scrambled aboard, his hands feet and clothes daubing more gore on the sticky paint.

"It's set. Five minutes. I'd have been back sooner but there was stuff bouncing all over the place out there."

The turret gun blasted off behind Revell and punished his ears. Derelict machinery in an open front tractor shed sparkled as the bullets struck sparks from it. A body flopped down from the rafters, and a full burst into the roof brought down three more and started a fire among the shattered timber.

An anti-tank rocket soared from the corner of a much-holed barn. Revell just had time to duck before it struck. It impacted low on the hull, aft of the front wheel. The heat round blasted its jet of molten explosive into a box of reactive armor. With a roar the defensive charge exploded and disrupted the plasma stream, showering droplets of white hot material over the nearby bodies.

"It's OK, we just lost a wheel, we've plenty more." Revell acted fast to prevent a bail-out as the interior filled with smoke.

"It's buggered the power steering as well." Burke had to wrench hard at the wheel to get the ten-and-a-half tons of armored vehicle turning.

"Where's Hyde?" Finding the single periscope in the commander's hatch gave him virtually no vision closed down, Revell opened up and put his head out.

"He's off to our left. Looks like he's fine." Dooley had spotted the sergeant's eight-wheeler first, through the turret machine gun sight. "What the hell. Doesn't he know he's being followed?"

"Get us over there fast."

Holding on tight, Revell tried to see through the thickly swirling smoke as they bounced and jolted over a corner of what had been a deeply plowed field.

As they came alongside, Revell hailed his NCO. "This is a raid, not a looting expedition. Get your men out of those trucks."

Hyde shook his head. "No, it's refugees, hundreds of them. I've got another fifteen jammed inside here. Looks like the KGB were getting set to do another massacre."

"Let's move then. We've done all the damage we can."

A burst of machine gun fire raked the tall grass between the vehicles. Both turrets traversed and poured a barrage into the barn from which the rocket had come. Grenades burst flame and fragments against the structure, while the dashes of green tracer punched in through the thin walls.

From somewhere inside came a secondary explosion, and a burning figure tottered into the open, followed by another hidden by all-enveloping flame.

No more shots were aimed at them as the APCs

and trucks regained the road and started for the cover of the woods. Revell was looking up from his watch, at the farm when the charges aboard the pick-up detonated.

Chapter 26

A huge bubble of flame soared high above the cluster of buildings. The farmhouse itself appeared to bulge outward, dust and smoke spurting from every opening. Its walls disintegrated and the roof, stripped of many of its tiles, collapsed straight down into the ruin.

To Revell it appeared to happen in complete silence, then the report and shock wave swept across the fields, blinding him with a storm of dirt and grass seeds.

Hyde's APC was already among the trees, with the lead trucks, when mortar shells began to fall along the tree line. A bomb struck a bough above the column and sent a hail of fragments through the thin bodywork of an old Zil radio van. It ran off the road and tipped slowly onto its side as the wheels struck a ditch.

An avalanche of screaming women poured through the rear doors as they burst open. Those unhurt threw themselves at the other trucks squeezing past the wreck. Others lay still or squirmed gently, clutching at gaping wounds.

With more of the mortar rounds blasting the edge of the woods, Revell had his crew dismount to load the injured onto the roof of the APC.

"Where's that stupid old cow going." Dooley spotted an elderly woman wandering away into the trees. He started after her.

The bomb that hit her must have been a freak direct hit, as it burst above the ground. The smoke drifted clear to reveal only half a torso, with lacerated legs still attached.

Several of those hauled onto the harsh metal of the armored personnel carrier were clearly dying from their massive head wounds. Their mouths hung slack and they were deeply unconscious.

As they drove into the woods more shells landed, straddling where they had been parked, riddling the overturned truck with thousands of slivers of steel and setting it ablaze.

Thick black smoke blotted out the road and their last view of the farm. Revell was not sorry to see the last of it. The stench from the civilians in and on the APC was almost overpowering. Blood was everywhere. It congealed on the metal, stiffened on his clothes, coated his face and hands.

They reduced speed to a crawl while he tried to bind field-dressings over the worst of the wounds he could reach. When they reached the spot where the pioneers waited to activate the mines for the road block, there was no room for them to board. After switching on the seismic, infra-red and other devices they had to jog alongside.

For a brief moment Revell felt relief flood through his body. They were safe now from pursuit, at least by land. It was unlikely that under the prevailing conditions the enemy would put helicopters into the air to seek them out; still it was a risk and he had a sky-watch maintained.

"How many of the shits do you reckon we hit, Major?"

Ripper stuck his head up through a hatch, gulping in the comparatively untainted air.

"I wasn't keeping a count, but it must be a couple of hundred we knocked out. It was almost too easy."

"Wouldn't have been if they'd got that flak gun into action. Clarence did a good job there. I saw him blow the gunner's head clean off. Hell of a shot. Is he starting back now?"

"Should be on his way."

The sniper reloaded, pushing the two empty magazines forward and out of his way. He was picking his targets with care, isolated men whose death would not be easily attributable to fire from any particular direction.

In several cases the bodies of his victims lay undiscovered fifteen minutes after he had put them down. That was not so surprising though, the whole area was littered with dead and wounded.

Such rescue work as was going on appeared totally uncoordinated, most of the effort being centered on the ruins of the farmhouse.

Clarence readjusted his ear plugs. The report of

the Barrett's firing was vicious in the confined space of his dug-out. He could be certain though, that at the target it would be completely inaudible. Death was coming to his targets with silent violence.

The activity about the farmhouse increased. It was tempting to put several bullets into the group. He could do it, and pull out fast, long before they could zero in on his position. But he wanted a better target.

It appeared that a body was being pulled out. It was a wounded man. Through his sight the sniper saw an arm move as he was lifted onto a litter.

A sudden furious motion among the drifting smoke brought his attention to a helicopter that was coming in to a fast landing.

It touched down, bouncing once before settling. A solitary figure jumped out and made toward the farm.

Tracking him, Clarence knew he was moving too quickly for a shot. Still following him, he unclipped the magazine, ejected the round in the breech, and by touch alone replaced it with one that held armor-piercing high explosive incendiary shells.

He reached the group by the litter. They fell back instantly as he strode among them.

The man on the ground stirred, appeared to be attempting to push himself to a sitting position. Clarence clearly saw him extend his arm toward the newcomer, as if to fend something off.

A flurry of action too swift at the distance for the sniper to follow, and then the figure on the ground arched, and collapsed back.

What on earth was happening? It was like watching an obscure mime show, with the story-line unknown and the characters barely glimpsed.

Striding back toward the helicopter, the man performed a familiar action. Even at that distance it could be recognized. He was holstering a pistol.

"Rastrelnikov." Clarence knew the word well. It was one that all Russians, all members of the Warsaw Pact forces avoided mentioning. He had heard of such men. Theirs was the task of bringing instant punishment to Warpac commanders and officers who had failed. Rastrelnikov, the executioner.

Still he was moving too fast for a safe shot. Panning ahead, Clarence aligned his sights on the helicopter's pilot, sat in the cockpit directly facing the hideout. He did not have to look to see the killer reboard, he saw the little three seater bounce on its spindly tricycle undercarriage.

Nor did he need to be able to hear the change in engine note to know the aircraft was about to lift off. The reflection of the sun on the windshield shimmered as the blades rotated faster.

It was obviously a very old machine. He had to rack his brain to recall the NATO designation for it. Hare, that was it. Yes, three seater, no armor, no armorment. The fuel tank was set high up, close behind the engine.

If he missed the pilot with his first shot, he would use the rest of the magazine's contents to rake the fuselage in that general area.

Suddenly it was lifting, almost catching him off guard. And as it did it was swinging round. He was losing his view of the cockpit.

When it was thirty feet up Clarence snapped a single shot at the cockpit side window. The weapon kicked back hard against his shoulder. Damn! A miss. Must have allowed too much lead. The chopper was climbing still, and beginning to pick up forward speed, its nose tilting downward.

Again he fired and this time kept firing. He saw strikes on the rear starboard quarter, about where the fuel should be. A single shot went slightly wide, smacking into the base of the rotors.

Then he could only watch as it continued to gain height and move across in front of him. Without warning the helicopter yawed violently, practically going into a roll. The rotors were breaking from the hub, filling the sky with whirling blades of metal.

It fell like a stone, the tail boom distorting and almost breaking away before the chopper hit the meadow. The fuselage burst in a shower of torn panels, telescoping to half its length.

A truck bumped out of the farm toward the crash site. Before it was halfway there, smoke began to filter from the crushed cockpit. An instant later fire raged across the wreckage, starting secondary blazes among the surrounding swaths of wild barley.

Habit, almost amounting to instinct, caused Clarence to replace the magazine and methodically pump carefully aimed shots at the vehicle and its passengers.

The truck stalled. Leaving two men dead in the cab, those riding on the open back jumped off and dove underneath for cover.

At that range, fifteen hundred meters, the sniper knew his bullets could pass clean through the truck's chassis and still find them. Or he could flush them into the open by igniting the gas tank. But he didn't.

He had, quite simply, had enough of killing. Pushing the rifle to one side, he stretched out and turned over on his back. It was good to at last take the pressure off his elbows, and to straighten the crick in his back, neck and shoulders. Almost as an afterthought, he removed his earplugs.

By now the sun would almost have set behind the hills. Very little light was finding its way in. He lay there, in the semi-darkness, trying to come to a decision he knew he could no longer put off.

Chapter 27

"Anybody care to explain what's happening here?" Revell left it to Sampson and some of the pioneers to carefully remove the casualties from the top of the APCs. The unloading of the stunned and bewildered refugees from the trucks he delegated to Sergeant Hyde.

Close to the children's graveyard was parked an immaculate M-34, two-and-a-half-ton truck. Revell didn't have to look at its insignia to know to what outfit it belonged. Standing in front of it were twenty MPs. In front of them, a pile of new pick handles.

Lieutenant Vokes had them covered with his pistol. He was flanked by two of his men holding levelled SA-80s, and Old William with his shovel.

With his Walther, Vokes waved forward a big sergeant from among the group.

Revell recognized his face from the earlier incident. "Ball seems to be in your court."

"We've been threatened. We are now. You're a witness."

Selecting a pick handle, Revell hefted it, and made an experimental swing. "Nice of you to bring us these. That's what they are, isn't it? Presents?"

"My men were attacked last time. They were for our self-protection."

The sergeant was almost purple with suppressed fury at his situation. "We came here to take you in, under close arrest."

"What's the charge?"

"You got all day?"

"Major," Vokes had been listening intently to the conversation. "If you go with these men, I believe something will happen to you on the way to headquarters."

"I won't be going with them."

"Going to do a runner?"

Revell read the contempt on the sergeant's face, and then wiped it off. "I'm going in OK, but not with you. For two reasons. First, like my lieutenant says, there's a chance I might be in less than perfect health by the time I get there, if I do. Second, your transport has been commandeered."

"The hell it has, who by?"

"Me. We've got wounded civilians here. Your truck is just the right size to take them in comfort, of a sort. You and these other thugs can walk. I'll give you an armed escort part of the way. To see you come to no harm, naturally. I'd get going right away if I were you. It's going to be as black as hell tonight. My men have torches but I doubt they'll lend them to you."

"I'll herd them, Major." Carrington pushed himself forward. "I haven't forgotten that crack about baby killers."

"OK, take three men with you. Ride in one of the APCs, and set a fast pace. I don't want these specimens in these parts a moment longer than necessary. About six kilometers should give them a good workout."

For a moment it looked as if the MPs were considering non-cooperation, then they saw the faces of their escorts and thought otherwise.

"Get the injured on board. I'll hitch a ride with them."

"You want your own escort, Major?"

Revell declined Dooley's offer, and a dozen more from others as he got his kit together. While he was gathering and packing it he noticed Andrea watching. Already she had changed back into battledress. He was jamming the last items into a borrowed kitbat when she sauntered over.

"You watched me, in the woods?"

"I hadn't intended to, but when I saw what you were doing . . ."

"You saw everything?"

"Yes."

"When, if you come back, I will do it again, for you to watch. You will enjoy that, as you enjoyed the last time."

Her hand sought and found his erection. She

squeezed it hard, trying to hurt, failing because of the thick folds of material. "Perhaps I will let you help me. Perhaps."

He said nothing. There was nothing he could say. Did he hate her or love her? Shit, as if he didn't have enough on his mind.

Try as he did though, full as he was of worries about the situation he'd got himself into, he couldn't get her out of his thoughts. From the cab of the truck, as it pulled out, she was the last one he saw.

"I don't like you, Major Revell." The general leaned back in his chair, sucking hard on his pipe as he applied a match. "You shouldn't be in the army. You should be out their wandering the Zone with one of those renegade bands. Orders mean nothing to you. Discipline means about the same. You boss, because you certainly don't command, you boss a rag-tag outfit of misfits who wouldn't last five minutes in a decent military unit."

"A lot of soldiers wouldn't last five minutes in my combat company, general."

"Always the smart answer. Well let's hear your smart answer to this one. How did we find out so fast that you were pulling a stunt? You'll never guess. We got it from the Reds. That's it, they spotted it on satellite before the 717th could report in themselves. Not nice finding that out from them. Spoiled the President's day, sort of."

"Are they breaking the truce?"

"What the hell do you care? You know why it spoiled the President's day? Because he was on the hot line yesterday. Seems 'I' Corp had put that file of yours and the films into a real special package. Yesterday they made a present of it to the Reds, with a note saying we'd show it to the up-coming Conference of Neutral Nations. The Reds don't need any more bad press at the moment, especially not while those gents are in meeting. So we were going to hold it over them, get some sort of useful deal out of them. One that would be in our favor."

"What sort of deal?"

"How the hell should I know. I don't get invited to the White House that often. I'm told we'd have got something we wanted real bad. Would have got it too, whatever it was, only your raid screwed us up. The Russians are saying that if we forget those graves, they'll forget the raid. Seems they weren't that keen on that character Tarkovski, any more than we were. Word is, they're going to take care of him, if you haven't yet."

"So in the eyes of everyone, our knocking about a KGB punishment battalion who are known to be guilty of mass murder and worse, is about the equivalent of their war crimes against a few thousand civilians. Men, women and children."

"You play with words all you want. If I were you I wouldn't buck it. It's got your nuts out of the fire. But don't you go thinking you've got off."

Puffing vigorously at his pipe, the general walked to the window. "It's not my decision, but all charges against you are to be dropped. You keep your rank and your command."

"There has to be a catch."

"You're damned right there is. You and your cruds like the Zone, so in the Zone you're going to stay. You think in the past you've had nasty missions, they ain't nothing to what's being dreamed up for you at this moment. And to give you an idea of the thinking about your company, I'll tell you right here, the first thing you're getting is a week's leave for every last man. And not just with some shitty rest camp with a flea-bitten cinema and two bathrooms. No, you're being dumped outside the Zone for seven whole days. Guess why."

"You're hoping we'll get desertions."

"Got it in one. If it isn't convenient to disband you, we'll let you wither away. What's left after you get back are going to be hurling from one hot spot to another. If there's anyone of you left after six months I'll be amazed, and maybe a touch disappointed."

"Is that it, General?" Revell had heard such promises made before. This one he was more inclined to take seriously.

"That's it. Consider yourself lucky it's worked out this way. I'd have done it differently."

"And the Communists get away with the murder of those civilians."

"Let it go, Major. You're in a league you don't know anything about, in way over your head. There's nothing you can do anymore. You had your fun, you slapped the Reds' wrist, it's over. And don't go getting any ideas about peddling your copies of those reports among the press boys here. That's been taken care of. None of them want to lose accreditation. And as for the television crews . . . you know them, if it isn't here and now and in color then they don't want to know. There isn't anybody else to sneak it to. The story is as dead as those civvies."

Chapter 28

Before leaving the headquarters building, Revell went to the men's room. As he washed his hands he saw his face in the mirror. The splashes of blood, now dried and flaking, couldn't hide the stress lines around his eyes, or the bags beneath them.

Another officer came in and stood at the next basin, scrubbing ingrained ink stains from his fingers. It took a moment to click, then he recognized Captain Porter.

"I've got it."

Porter was almost dancing with excitement. "I've got my discharge, medical grounds. I'd never thought of that. A sergeant suggested it."

"Rather quick, wasn't it?" Revell knew it could take months before you came before a Board. He'd watched every stage of Dooley's several attempts, becoming quite an authority on the subject in the process.

"Is it? The sergeant arranged it all. He has a friend . . ."

"Must have cost a lot."

Porter reddened and tried to laugh the suggestion off.

"So what now? Back to the States, and teaching?" He'd dried his hands, and would have left, but Porter was in the narrow doorway.

"Oh no. That's not my only stroke of luck. That county paper, I told you about. Well they've offered me a position. Not exactly as a reporter. More sort of an office post, in editorial, but of course I'll still be able to submit stories. Who knows, perhaps one of them will get picked up by a national. That does happen, you know."

"When do you go home?" Suddenly Revell was not in a hurry.

"As soon as I can get a flight. Within a week I should imagine."

"Give me your address. There's something I can send you."

Producing a very professional looking notebook, Porter jotted it down and handed it over. "Is it a story? I mean, rather out of the ordinary. Hope you don't mind my asking, but so many I speak to, when I mention I write, they think I can get their memoirs published . . ."

"It's a story."

"Oh good. I do hope it gets me a by-line."

"I should think there's a very good chance it'll surprise you."

Stepping out into the blacked out street, Revell felt a great weight had been lifted from him. He felt the piece of paper in his hand. Carefully he folded it and pushed it to the bottom of an inside pocket.

The town was a miserable one, just inside the western fringe of the Zone, but for Revell it was a great place. As he walked in search of a ride back to his unit he felt really light and carefree. Yes, this was a great town. It was good to be alive.

It was pitch black. Only the luminous dial of his watch was visible in the trench. Clarence watched the fires at the farm. Many times he saw figures clearly silhouetted against the flames, but he never touched his rifle. Among the burning ruin of the farmhouse he could see the outline of a flak-gun, canted over at a crazy angle.

A huge barn was emitting vast showers of sparks that started hundreds of secondary fires in the fields. Some of them would merge, and for a brief while a line of fire would snake along in the distant darkness.

He couldn't be certain under these conditions, but he got the impression that objects were being thrown into some of the fires. That didn't make sense, unless it was the bodies of their dead they were disposing of in so convenient and labor saving a manner.

All sense of time had been lost, and it didn't matter. Clarence felt for the satchel he had brought with him. Carefully he emptied its contents, sorted them by feel, and arranged them along the floor of the excavation.

Strange that for so long he had been obsessive about cleanliness, and here he was, content to remain in this unlined scrape. It was like lying at the bottom of a grave, without benefit of the decency of a lined casket.

By now he would be posted as missing. They might come out and search, but he'd been careful to separate from his escort a considerable distance away from the site he had finally chosen.

All the months and years of killing were almost over. He felt as if he were burned out. Burned out . . . how appropriate.

The Browning Hi-Power was heavy in his hand, its checkered wooden grips warm against his palm. He had to turn on his side.

With his free hand he groped for the metal canister wedged between the breech of the rifle and the wall of the trench. He slipped his middle finger through the dangling ring at its top.

Strangely, Clarence realized that he felt no fear, no emotion of any sort. He had handed out death so many times. Always with a cool, calm precision. This was only one more, to be handled with the same methodical patience.

Slowly he withdrew the pin from the thermite demolition grenade. Satisfied it was out, he placed the end of the barrel of the pistol in his mouth and squeezed the trigger steadily.

Unrecognized by those who held his arms and legs, the broken corpse of Colonel Tarkovski was swung back and forth, and then into the burning barn. Blazing bales tumbled down and hid his remains from sight.

On a hillside above the farm there was a brief flare of bright light. It passed unnoticed.

ASHES
by William W. Johnstone

OUT OF THE ASHES (1137, $3.50)
Ben Raines hadn't looked forward to the War, but he knew it was coming. After the balloons went up, Ben was one of the survivors, fighting his way across the country, searching for his family, and leading a band of new pioneers attempting to bring American OUT OF THE ASHES.

FIRE IN THE ASHES (2669, $3.95)
It's 1999 and the world as we know it no longer exists. Ben Raines, leader of the Resistance, must regroup his rebels and prep them for bloody guerrilla war. But are they ready to face an even fiercer foe—the human mutants threatening to overpower the world!

ANARCHY IN THE ASHES (2592, $3.95)
Out of the smoldering nuclear wreckage of World War III, [illegible] Raines has emerged as the strong leader the Resistance needs. When Sam Hartline, the mercenary, joins forces with an invading army of Russians, Ben and his people raise a bloody banner of defiance to defend earth's last bastion of freedom.

SMOKE FROM THE ASHES (2191, $3.50)
Swarming across America's Southern tier march the avenging soldiers of Libyan blood terrorist Khamsin. Lurking in the blackened ruins of once-great cities are the mutant Night People, crazed killers of all who dare enter their domain. Only Ben Raines, his son Buddy, and a handful of Ben's Rebel Army remain to strike a blow for the survival of America and the future of the free world!

ALONE IN THE ASHES (2591, $3.95)
In this hellish new world there are human animals and Ben Raines—famed soldier and survival expert—soon becomes their hunted prey. He desperately tries to stay one step ahead of death but no one can survive ALONE IN THE ASHES.

Available wherever paperbacks are sold, or order direct from the Publisher. Send cover price plus 50¢ per copy for mailing and handling to Zebra Books, Dept. 2633, 475 Park Avenue South, New York, N.Y. 10016. Residents of New York, New Jersey and Pennsylvania must include sales tax. DO NOT SEND CASH.